VOODOO MAN

A DCI Harry Morgan Thriller

Keith Lawson

First published in Great Britain in 2021 by Amazon

ISBN: 9798456069917

I control my empire through fear.
People have to know there is punishment
if they cross me.

I am OBEAH.

CHAPTER 1

Social housing – an ambitious name for where I was this evening. No doubt there are many families in the neighbourhood who are decent, honest folk, but there are always a number of scumbags, workshy, benefit-cheating scumbags, who slip in among them, and dodgy letting agencies who provide poor accommodation, and ratbag landlords who refuse to invest in their buildings. This place looked like a mix – people who tried to make their neighbourhood look better and vandals who took down every effort eventually. Even at this hour, there were kids on bikes hovering on the fringes of the operation, effing at the constables.

The blue lights flashing off buildings and leaf-free trees had directed me down a road to a collection of flats around a cul-de-sac. Looking at the shoddy exteriors of the buildings I thought "Dead end is about right." A broken bicycle, wheel misshapen, was hanging from one tree. A soiled mattress leaned unceremoniously against a wall, as if it had thrown itself there in an act of suicide. Light shone from windows as residents kept their curtains open so they could see the drama on their doorsteps, we were outdoing TV tonight for viewing figures. I am never comfortable that, in one of the world's richest nations, we allow poverty to exist like this.

I drew up to the police cordon, parked my Beamer and got out. Squad cars, silently strobing blue light off the walls, a white unmarked Forensics van at the forefront, and two ordinary vehicles that I recognised as the transport of my team members.

"Chief Inspector Morgan," I said to the copper guarding the ribbon of crime-scene tape stretching from lamppost to vandalised tree, showing him my ID. He raised it so I didn't have to stoop too low to get under and recorded my arrival on a clipboard. I nodded then walked up the path to the activity around the entrance of one block of flats.

My sergeant – Andy Robins, known as 'Andy Pandy' for his baby looks and devotion to vertically striped shirts – looked up from his notebook whilst stood in the doorway where he had been awaiting my arrival.

"Hi, boss. Got dead woman in 16, looks like murder. Rope round her neck and knife in her chest."

Andy was not being funny. Until the post-mortem ruled cause of death, he would not make assumptions. After all, this could be a suicide made to look like murder for insurance, although it was more normal to try to make a murder look like suicide if not like accidental death. As a team, we valued Method over Inspiration.

"OK to go in?" I asked.

"Yeah, but you'll need to suit up; Forensics still working. Kits outside number 12 – that's the perimeter for evidence."

Crime Scene Investigators maintain a safe distance from the incident so that the chance of mucking up evidence was reduced. I went inside, leaving Andy to do what he does well, organise the uniforms to go flat-to-flat and house-to-house to find out the background of the resident or residents of number 16. If she had a partner, he, or she, would be prime suspect. Statistically, the victim typically knows his or her attacker and serial killers and psychopaths are usually the stuff of novels, especially here in Dorset.

I rummaged for a large size zip-up and donned it. Then the booties, gloves and mask. People think the mask is to protect us from inhaling unpleasants, smells and such, but is actually meant to prevent us contaminating a scene with our body fluids – sneeze droplets, saliva spray and the like. Barely one hundred years ago, fingerprints were the big breakthrough. Today our evidence can be microscopic.

I entered flat 16, using the 'stepping stones' –steel platforms on tiny feet, big enough to prevent our size 10s touching the floor. They get sterilised between uses so they don't cross-contaminate crime scenes; but if they get damaged then a local scrap merchant gets our business. The flat smelt surprisingly fresh. I was expecting the more usual smells of cooking that lingered, because these places had no cooker hoods filtering the odours to the outside. Instead I thought my olfactory senses were picking up incense or scented candles, even through the mask. Then again, I did believe my sense of smell had improved since I gave up smoking or, as the alcoholics say about their addiction, "giving up" .

There were a number of 'snowmen' in the flat, I made the fourth in my white crime-suit, but I recognised the tubby shape of Alex Dawson easily, him being only five foot five.

"Daws," I said, to get his attention.

"Harry," he acknowledged. "Body's in the bedroom," nodding over to his left.

There was the body of a naked woman, late twenties, early thirties, in a bed. Not overweight, slim from diet or drug user slim, not gym fit but well-proportioned for height. Small breasts, even allowing for her being laid down and gravity pulling them into her body and to her side. Her legs were crossed at the ankles and her arms stretched directly away from the body n the crucifix position. A cord around her neck, tight, and a kitchen knife stood upright from her chest., no other sign of a wound visible. A lack of visible blood on the body or bedsheet.

"Minimal bleed from the knife wound. Done after death?" I enquired of Daws.

"Likely so, but I'll know for sure when we get her in the mortuary. Probable cause is the rope round her neck. I can see haemorrhaging in the eyes to indicate strangulation."

"Lived alone," said Andy Robins, who had come in behind me. "First neighbours say single woman but with lots of male visitors. One of them called it in when they noticed her front door wide open and looked in."

I pulled open the drawer of a bedside cabinet, revealing packets of condoms and a vibrator. Gave Andy a look and got a response in kind – on the game'.

I took a long, slow look around the room. "Black sheet, black candles. A bit Gothic, along with her tatts and piercings."

"Pretend more than serious," Andy made a comment. "Boxed sets of Twilight and Buffy among others, in the living room."

"So we rule out Satanic sacrifice," I offered, deadpan.

"Not if the papers get this," replied Daws, holding up a black cockerel in an evidence bag. Its throat had been cut and it was almost decapitated.

"Blood anywhere?"

"Not that we can find."

"So killed elsewhere and brought here? Serious contribution or to confuse us?"

"Where do you get a black cock round here?" asked a young constable, causing us to fold over laughing. Yes, real childish, but humour helps us deal with the nastiness. When I recovered, I gave orders.

"Check the fresh meat places, local butchers, not supermarkets. No joy, take a larger circle, along public transport routes and arterial roads out to the countryside."

Andy pitched in. "Do a bit of Googling first. We've a lot of countryside and farming, even before we consider the New Forest. Maybe identify the breed and see if rare or what."

"What he said," was my contribution.

I went outside and looked for Sergeant Petra Polanski. Spotted her on the perimeter and when she saw me approaching she reached into her squad car, pulled out a flask and poured me a black coffee with lots of sugar. As well as a damned good copper, Polly was the mother of the unit. She thought about how to make things better on jobs like this and remove as much discomfort as possible. Everyone chipped in a few quid at month end and she would stock up on biscuits, tea and coffee. We didn't run to a catering wagon like some forces but this was nicer in our eyes. We were a unit. I had the impression that Polly "would", but I didn't want to ruin a good working relationship and atmosphere by playing at home. She was what some people call "fit"; I wouldn't disagree, with her natural blonde looks and startling blue eyes added to an athletic figure.

"You're a life saver as usual, Polly."

"Caffeine is better than nicotine, boss."

Andy Pandy came out the house, stowing his notebook away in an inside pocket and drawing his coat closer against the cold of the night, after he shed the whites.

"Got one of those for me, Poll?"

8

"You're behind on your subs, Andy. You missed last month."

I chipped in. "Go on, Poll. He'll being getting loads of overtime from this."

"I didn't say he couldn't have a drink. Just reminding him."

"Bless you, Poll. " Andy gratefully took a cup, blowing off the steam. We used to wonder how long prior Polly could make up her flasks and the drinks were never less than hot.

"Initial thoughts, Andy."

He paused to gather his thoughts before speaking. Andy was always measured.

"Prostitute, drug user – needle marks on arm. Not a dissatisfied customer – no anger in the act or staging. Premeditated perhaps; brought props with him. Knife doesn't match any in the kitchen and they are a set, not a collection of odds. We'll check if her prints are on it, but it's probably wiped. The cockerel is a turn up. That took some effort – to obtain, kill it and bring the corpse here. A bit of set dressing that wouldn't be necessary for playacting; makes this look a bit more serious."

"I agree."

"We'll have uniform door to door first thing. See what the neighbours know. Tomorrow we'll check her prints – see if she is in the system. Not found anything in the house with a name on it yet. Her landlords may know, unless she is an unofficial sublet."

"If she's on the game, and indications are she is, she has to advertise and be contactable. Any sign of a phone?"

"Again, nothing. Likely the perp took it away as it may have clues – his phone number perhaps."

"Get uniform to check the area for a throwaway., especially bins. Ask the Drug Squad about what goes on around here. Might be able to find her dealer."

"I'll get on that," Polly offered.

"Well, I think our work here is done for the night. We'll let uniform keep the site safe and let Forensics get on with their work. Briefing at ten tomorrow at the station. Let the team know, Andy, then get home."

Andy nodded and headed back to share the instruction. I handed Polly my empty cup back, kissed her on the cheek.

"Night, Poll. Get some sleep. See you in the morning."

Despite this being a low murder rate county, mostly aggro deaths after drink or drugs or marital, we'd had enough experience together to function efficiently. I only needed a light hand on the tiller as it were, all my people knew their roles and were supportive of each other. My role was often about authorising actions over and above and negotiating upstairs for overtime and better kit. I headed home to Lower Parkstone. The work would start tomorrow and be intensive until we caught the perpetrator, then be ready for the trial.

At this time, we had no idea how things would turn out or the personal cost.

CHAPTER 2

Home is a flat in Lower Parkstone. The area has a urban village feel, despite the heavy traffic running through it. A green park with an ornate fountain centres it, squirrels run around, a boules club meet there. Around it are independent cafes, all doing decent coffee, an artisan baker, a few bars, and small businesses.

I lived alone since Lorraine, my wife died. Drunk driver crashed into her one evening as she was coming home from work. Not needing a big place and down to one income, I sold our house and bought this flat, mortgage free. Comfortable and I didn't need to be doing lots of housework.

Feeling hungry, I checked the fridge when I got in; realised I needed to go shopping. Made a bowl of Weetabix so as not to go to bed with a growling stomach. Caught up on an episode of The Walking Dead then hit the sack. Dreamed of zombies, that will teach me.

I was in work early. The others hadn't arrived. That was OK after a late night case. I preferred they all got a decent rest and not to come in half dead with fatigue. I could get by on a little sleep, fortified by coffee throughout the day. Checked emails. Nothing pressing except a request from the Prosecutor to meet up to discuss a trial coming up at Crown Court where I had to give testimony. I sent an acknowledgement, agreeing to phone him later.

Polly was the first in. I heard her arrive and set up the coffee machine. I had bought it for the office to get us off instant muck. She would know I was in and I could expect the first cup as soon as the brew was ready. Most of us drank black but a couple would bring in those little plastic cups of UHT milk, usually "acquired" from the training room rather than bought.

Hearing Andy arrive and say "Hi" to Polly, I opened my door.

"Andy!"

"Yes, boss."

"Any keys at the house? Can you remember."

"I didn't notice any. I'll ask Forensics and check the evidence bags."

"Thanks. Was on my mind that I hadn't seen keys. It might not be her house. We might have things back to front and she was invited there then murdered. She might not be the woman occupant the neighbours know."

Polly handed me my coffee. "No, she lived there. Everything said she is the woman occupant. Her shade of lipstick matches the stick in the bathroom. Her size clothes in the wardrobe."

"See. That's why we need you, Poll."

Polly extended her middle finger on her way back to the coffee machine. The rest of the gang started arriving. I waited until everyone was in, got their drinks and seated.

"Right. Unusual murder. Let's tick off what needs doing."

I went through a list and hands went up, accepting the tasks. We needed to identify the victim, either by her prints or the letting agency/landlords, best if both concur. Uniform would be doing door-by-door today. Will need to meet them for debriefing and collecting their notes.
Traffic cams around the district to see if what vehicles were about. Handy to have post-mortem results for time of death. Any results from Forensics,

12

e.g. fingerprints, blood samples not from the victim, but that will be slow; I can't get fast track for the death of a prossie on our budgets.

"The Satanic setting. For real? To send us off on a wild goose chase? Or a warning to somebody?"

Andy interjected. "I did some Googling before breakfast. Found a specialist poultry farmer in West Dorset where the cockerel could have come from, so I phoned him and, guess what? He had a break in and lost a cockerel, no hens. Dorchester nick is sending over the crime report today."

"Good work, Andy. That makes it interesting. The cockerel was acquired and not a find. If it is the same animal then we have planning before the visit. Let's keep this out the papers for now. Don't want lurid headlines getting in our way. OK. Get stuck in. Any breakthroughs, I want to know immediately. Otherwise, we'll meet again at four o'clock to update."

I turned to Andy. "I'd better go and brief Upstairs."

I knocked on the door of the big boss, Sharon MacKay, and waited for "Come in" , which wasn't instant, her usual delay to suggest "I'm busy. Wait 'til I'm ready". When it did come I stood outside waiting for a repeat entreaty to enter. Power play pisses me off so I don't follow their rules.

"Come in!" louder.

"Morning, ma'am. If you haven't heard, we had a murder last night over Boscombe. Young woman, probably on the game."

"Drug addict as well, no doubt. Well, don't take too long wrapping this up. It will be her pimp or another druggie."

"Might be more complicated than that." I filled her in on the scenario. She didn't like it; I could see £ signs in her eyes. This could mess up her budgets. When she'd been an Inspector, she'd been a good copper, but high promotion meant that what mattered was reputation and budgets because that was all her superiors were interested in. She was the perfect example of the Peter Principle if you expected good coppers to become good administrators. We'd started at the same time but she knew office politics and how to smooze.

"OK, Harry. Try to keep it simple and don't let the overtime run away. We've had our budgets cut again."

"The force gets enough free hours off the guys. They deserve to be paid properly."

"Reality and fairness aren't always on the same team. Well, that's it for now. Make sure you inform me when you make some progress."

I snapped to attention in mockery but her head was in her paperwork and she didn't notice.

I left the room, craving a cigarette but this was week 3 and I was determined to see it through. Talking to the Prosecutor would be a distraction and there was an attractive secretary just commenced work and the word was she was single. I was getting itchy.

The Prosecutor confirmed he could see me so I headed straight over. The CPS is a Wessex wide organisation, covering Dorset, Hampshire, Isle of Wight and Wiltshire, based in Eastleigh. I didn't have to travel that far though. We arranged to meet at the Court by the Royal Bournemouth Hospital.

Tom Williams and I had worked together before. He was good at his job and had a good conviction rate. It helped that he spent time with officers before to check the evidence and for early warnings of any potential pitfall.

In this instance, I'd stumbled across a drugrunner while doing a cover shift as a favour and we arrested him with drugs in the boot of his car. He had previous, and he coughed for a plea if he got a lighter sentence. There was a chance he'd spill on others and point us at the ringleader. I'd rather he went down for a long time but compromises have to be made under weakened resources and budget cuts. I'd argue that the effort to stick him inside for longer would save us another trial down the line as he was a serial offender and would resume as soon as free but targets to be met, etc. etc. and it's the path of least resistance approach.

The secretary was a looker...but she had an engagement ring on her finger. Consolation was leaving my car at the court and walking down the road to the hotel, which had a cafe for non-residents. My phone rang as I was walking.

"Morgan."

"Boss," it was Andy. " Plod collected the neighbours' accounts and she moved in 6 months ago with a bloke. They say he's not been around for a few weeks. It does appear to be the woman from their descriptions, so not a visitor."

"Right. Well, boyfriend-stroke-pimp is a person of interest.. Find out what you can and let's see if he has a record."

"Already on it."

"Good man. Have you heard from Daws what time the post-mortem?"

"Two o'clock."

"OK. I'll make my way there then come back to the office."

"How'd the meeting go on the smuggler?"

"They're accepting his plea for a lighter sentence."

I could hear Andy's unspoken disgust.

"Sometimes I wonder if it's worth the trouble of arresting them. It's fucking revolving doors and while he's off the streets someone else will takeover."

"And we'll catch them. It's what we do."

"I'll get on with tracking the boyfriend. Speak later."

"Yeah. Bye."

I had a double espresso at the cafe, passed on a pastry, and watched the clientele. Most were drop-ins. We had the Courts almost next door and the Royal Bournemouth Hospital across the road. It was also convenient for businessmen and women on the road, reps and the like. I phoned the local nick and told them where to send a car and a description of the purse thief working his trade. He stuck around a bit too long and the lads nicked him when he finally decided to leave. These are good venues for his work, one sees where the customer puts their purse or wallet after buying their drinks and ladies put their handbags on the floor or back of the chair, easily accessible to the thief. I didn't want to have to make a court appearance as a witness so I told the lads to make the booking based on a member of the public tip-off and the evidence on him.

CHAPTER 3

Alex Dawson was scrubbing up when I arrived and I joined him, not that I would be hands on, but one had to be as sure as possible at not cross-contaminating. He offered his menthol tin and I put some on my upper lip to mask the chemical and body spells we'd experience in the lab. He, on the other hand, never used the stuff. When I had once asked why, he said "Smells can be a clue. I can't shut down one of my senses." Daws was a true professional.

The purpose of the post-mortem was primarily to identify cause of death. Whatever the eye saw at the scene, we needed scientific evidence to help with the investigation and for a trial. What if the victim had had a heart attack at the sight of a weapon about to be applied? That would be death by natural causes and not murder under strict legal terms. We also learned about the lifestyle of the victim – health, drugs, diet – that could provide avenues of investigation and contacts.

I waited patiently at the side, not too close to the table, with my notebook. Daws would be dictating as he went and it would be picked up electronically as well as by video but I needed the salient points immediately for my team. On TV, the detective is always on to the pathologist - "Can you give me a time frame?". Well, once a time frame is stated it can come back and bite if wrong but the defence use the official first call to show a mistake and therefore "can we trust anything the forensic team say?" So, no pressure and lots of codicils for wriggle room later.

"We took a body temp at the scene, temp of the room and ambient temperature outside. The body was naked and uncovered but may have been covered between asphyxiation and the knife wound. Ally that to the low state of rigor mortis, we suggest a time frame of anything up to twelve hours before we arrived, but on probability about four hours previous."

Daws has given me the window but pointed me at the likelihood of the murder being only "four hours previous" and to concentrate on checking activity around the house and in nearby streets in the evening. I sent a text to Andy so he could organise the CCTV collection from traffic cams and any personal or business cameras in nearby streets. But as the perpetrator may have spent some time with the victim before killing her, his or her arrival time at the house could be much earlier. Initially, we'll be checking all movement away from the address and putting it into the database for pulling out later when we have more to go on.

Daws continued."No sexual activity, either vaginal, anal or oral. No semen, lubricants or spermicidal agents. Nor any saliva that is obvious should oral sex have taken place on the victim. We have tests that are more revealing but they take time so I'll confirm or update asap."

Daws was filling me in on the preliminary work he and his team had done in the morning. They would have done extensive external examinations; weight, height, body measurements, searches for bruises, marks and scars, fingernail scrapes, taking fingerprints, photographing finds.

"She wasn't killed by the knife. Stabbing, single wound, was post-mortem, hence the lack of blood flow. One straightforward incision by the

18

blade in a downward motion on a supine body. No hacking or other attempts to stab. So she was either unconscious or dead, and it's the latter all the evidence points to. Probably while she was on the bed; all the blood had pooled to her back regions, indicating she hadn't been moved after the kill, at least not far. Nor was she strangled by the cord. That was window dressing after manual strangulation. No fingerprints on the neck but we have bruising each side of the larynx that match a grip by two hands, a right and left, the thumbs go in deeper than the fingers. I will look for breaks in the cartilages of the larynx when I do the internal examination as extra confirmation. The usual haemorrhaging in the eyes from strangulation. We haven't identified any marks or abrasions to suggest she put up a struggle. I'll be looking for signs of how she might be been subdued prior to the killing."

Now we were going in on the body and internal examinations. He started with cutting open the body in a Y shape, shoulders to groin. I knew what happened next. The sawing out of ribs and breastbone, removal of organs for toxicology. There was nothing for me to remain for, thankfully, so I made my farewells and left, the sound of the electric saw cut off when the door closed behind me.

Some results would come through quickly – stomach contents for example, and whether any more bruising or wounds were revealed. Blows to the head are more visible when the scalp is removed. Samples will be taken from the organs to be sent to another lab for toxicology, which could be a week or more before we heard.

I stood outside the building and patted my pockets for my cigarettes before I remembered I was quitting. At one autopsy, I had seen the lungs of a heavy smoker and, added to my increasing shortness of breath, made the decision to quit. I was going cold turkey – no nicotine substitutes – as wanted to be totally free and not just switch my addiction. Someone suggested I try e-cigarettes, but what's the point?

I walked back to the Court to collect my car and drove back to the station. The canteen was doing pie and chips and breadpudding and custard, so I tucked in, remembering my fridge at the flat was nearly empty. Polly came in while I was eating and joined me at my table with her tea and salad. Salad! In autumn?

"OK, Harry?" We were less formal when off duty.

I pointed vaguely in the direction of her lips. "Mayo."

Polly wiped with a napkin and continued to eat. No talking shop when having lunch. Uncivilised and other ears around. Anyone might be leaking to a reporter or just showing off to friends in the pub later, then it ends up on social media and I have to go upstairs to explain what happened.

Pushing my empty pudding bowl aside to join the empty plate, this was another time I might have lit up, but I was helped by the law banning smoking indoors.

"Polly. Up to anything interesting other than work?"

"Pilates. Want to come?"

My face was the answer, which made Poll laugh.

"Stuck for what to do in down time, Harry?"

"Watching Netflix every night gets a bit boring by oneself. Can't be arsed to find a hobby."

"Andy would be grateful for a baby sitter. He and Maureen don't get out much."

"Not that good with kids, Poll."

20

"You haven't tried. Anyway, they'll be in bed by eight."

"And then I end up watching Netflix by myself?"

"Fancy swimming? Go well with your health kick."

I looked at the empty dishes and wondered why Polly thought I was on a health kick.

"Yeah, maybe. I'll think about getting some trunks."

I looked at my watch, a Bulova, a gift from my wife on my fortieth birthday and our tenth wedding anniversary. I missed her so much, but I missed sharing things even more. It's probably why I was the first in the office and last to leave most days. It was the companionship and hustle going on that filled the hours.

"Going back. See you in the office."

Poll nodded and opened a plain yoghurt she'd chosen for dessert. Maybe her discipline of diet and exercise for someone who was nearing 40 was how she kept her curves. The thought lingered until I shook it off and made my way to the office.

It was empty except for Detective Constable Phil Harding, who was managing the data boards. These are whiteboards on wheels onto which we write out info and magnetically pin photos and documents. It's a great boon to have everything available to see and move around as things develop. Harding was totally immersed in his tasks. I took a look at his progress and was satisfied at the job he was doing and gave a nod of approval. Harding was keen to please, as the newest arrival to the team, and very methodical. He retained a hint of the West Indian accent of his grandparents with an occasional Dorset burr. I felt he would be a real asset.

"I'll have a bit to add when we do the briefing at four."

I looked at my watch and saw it was 3.30 already and went into my room to check my notes and prepare a briefing.

Never did thin air seem so thin.

CHAPTER 4

The team assembled punctually, Andy Robins the last to arrive but looking excited, which I took to mean he had some prize nugget of info to share. I stood in front of the data boards. Harding had put up photos from the crime scene and drawn a time line, which yet needed detail apart from the body discovery.

"Pay attention, everyone. Victim was strangled manually. The cord and knife are window dressing or have some meaning to the killer or someone who learns of this. Bruising on the neck indicates it's likely a male by the spread but there are women with big hands so don't shut down your minds. Uniform have interviewed immediate neighbours and we believe this woman moved in with a male several months ago. He is a person of interest."

Andy was keen to catch my eye.

"Yes, Andy."

"The letting agency say the house was rented to a Martin Fox and his partner, Mariana Gosling. Fox hasn't been seen for a few weeks. Maybe he came home for some fun and things got out of hand."

The name meant something to me.

"Sorry, Andy. Rule him out. He has a perfect alibi....he's in custody and his trial comes up at month end. I was with CPS today discussing the case."

Andy was deflated only briefly.

"OK. Anyway, Mariana has a sheet. Possession and prostitution. We confirmed she is the victim when Path sent over her prints. I've copies to pass round. Look into her background and methodology for obtaining drugs and selling her body. We want pimps and pushers." Methodology is to investigate the victim and that may provided leads to the killer. Andy looked at me."Should we visit Fox and get some more info?"

I pondered. "Not just yet. Only if we get stuck. This is too close to his trial for smuggling and I don't want to complicate that. Let's she if she has any friends or family." I pulled my thoughts together and got back on track. "We don't know what time the killer arrived and how long after he, or she, murdered Mariana. Best estimate based on the forensics is that time of death is no longer than four hours before the neighbour noticed the open door. Can someone check back to see if the door was noticed earlier? That might give us a time frame for the killer leaving." Good to see volunteers. "Alison, I'll leave that with you. Polly. See if we can borrow some troops to check the CCTV from the neighbourhood and record traffic and pedestrians. Phil. Can you work with Polly and create one of your databases?"

Phil Harding was bit of a tech wizard. With the info on a database on the computer we could eliminate and also make a short list quite quickly, but it took time to create the database and enter everything. I knew what we ended up with would not be perfect but it would still be a tool and later might provide evidence for a trial.

"No problem. I'll record everything on two databases, one for motors and one for pedestrians. Motors will be by make and number . Comparing times of movement, we can eliminate straight past traffic and reduce the ist to those that enter the neighbourhood and don't leave for, what, an hour?"

"Sounds about right. The killer will need at least that. No signs of haste or struggle. An hour to enter, subdue Mariana, strangle her, lay her out and present her and leave. If he's risk-averse he won't have hung around."

Poll added. "There'll be a lot of traffic late afternoon, early evening. We'll have to look at each camera first for motorists then repeat for pedestrians."

"We'll need to get the camera footage in. Start in the morning. OK. Let's look at the scene and evidence collected. Phil. On the board if you please."

We looked at the crime scene photos while talking. Evidence had been bagged and recorded. Jobs allocated were to follow up on the cockerel Andy needed to chase for the incident report from Dorchester, which hadn't arrived as promised), the source of the knife (was it in the kitchen or did the killer bring it?), collate the search results of the vicinity to see if anything found, e.g. her phone, and to identify her phone number and trace it. Put out data into the national crime register to see if any similar crime in the UK.

As I dismissed the team to start on their tasks, I asked Polly into my office.

"Poll, When you get home tonight, do me a favour. Take your clothes off..." Her face registered amused disbelief. "No, listen. Take your clothes off and time how long before the pressure marks on the skin disappear. Come here." I invited her round to my side of the desk so she could see my computer screen with the picture of the dead woman. I zoomed in on

Mariana's chest.. "Look. No marks from a bra. How long does it take for skin to lose the marks? That could help with a time frame."

"OK, gov. But her little boobs may not take long, as for mine..."

"It's just a thought. Will you do it?"

"As long as you don't tell the team I was your test subject."

"Deal."

CHAPTER 5

I stayed late into the evening, sustained by the heavy lunch, the last of the coffee in the machine and a Mars bar I found in Andy's desk (mental note: buy some on way in tomorrow morning). It's alright to have the whiteboards and the files but you need to absorb the details so you can recall, match, notice things when out and about. Too much reliance on technology and not enough on the brain does not solve crimes. But, to assist the older brain, I took photos on my phone to refer to later if necessary.

Murder in Dorset usually was instant and violent – a domestic, a drunken brawl. Rare to have something planned and exotic. In my water, I felt a message was being sent, only I didn't know what. If we could identify the recipient, it might join up some of the dots.

Checking my watch, I could see it was 9.00 p.m.. I picked up the phone and called Ray Axel.

"Ray? It's Harry Morgan."

"Harry! Been a while. What's up?"

"Chance of a drink tonight? I'd like to pick your brains."

" A poor feast but, yeah, I'm good. Goat and Tricycle in twenty?"

"See you there."

Ray works drugs more than most crimes. He's the go-to-guy for info on the local scene. The victim was a drug user and we knew she injected rather than only smoked or sniffed, so Ray might have some names for me that I could have picked up and questioned. Also I needed the word on the street. The Goat and Tricycle was an easy walk for both of us and Ray chose it for the choice of real ales and craft beers, plus good grub. He beat me there and when I walked in, he called from a corner table with two bitters on it.

"Try this, Guest cask."

I followed the custom of not talking shop until we had had a couple of slow swallows, meditated on the flavour, and nodded our approval. A few of these and I'll have to leave my car at the station and ask for a blue-light taxi home (a friendly ride in a squad car, courtesy of uniform branch).

"How you keeping?"

"Not so bad, Ray. Polly is on to me to exercise."

"How is the gorgeous Polly? Missed a call from her."

"Heart and soul of the unit. Pity her man left her. Needs his head examined."

"If she ever wants to transfer, I'll find a position for her."

"Hands off. The day Polly leaves, the unit collapses and hell freezes over."

"So, what is it you need from me?"

Ray took a long drink from his glass, looking at me over the top. He wasn't a man to sip. I saw the hint to get a round in and went to the bar. I bought another pint for him but a single malt for myself.

"I've got a murdered prostitute who is also a mainstream drug user. Track marks on her arms. What's the business on the streets at the moment?"

"Nothing exceptional. The scene is active, particularly in certain areas. Typically, users buy a little extra to sell on to fund their habit. We've had the County Lines kids come down on the trains. Some users go on the game, men as well as women. Your vic a street girl or an at home?"

"Used a flat. Scene looked like it was set for a fetish and she had the condoms in the bedside drawer."

"A little out the ordinary. Home girls are generally a bit up market, have websites and use social media. Advertise as massage or therapists. A lot of our prostitution is streetside and off in the punter's car. Get someone on to the net and social media to see if she has a presence."

"Already on that. " Ray acknowledged with a nod. I continued, "Looking for the unusual. Not released to the press yet but she was strangled then a single stab wound in the chest. Positioned on the bed. All display and no passion."

"Hmm. Someone getting his kinks? Typical wannabe Rippers target prossies, but usually street girls. This one likes a bit of style and time. Particular details."

"Possibly. Not ruling it out. We'll learn from the National Crime Register if any similar crimes or this a first or one-off. The other thing....a black cockerel was left."

"That is a new signature. Part of the fetish or misdirection?"

"Too soon to tell. Just says he or she is a planner and organises ahead. That suggests a connection to the victim or at least some research to find a single woman willing to accommodate. Black sheets and candles. Did she have or did the crim bring them too?"

"Got your hands full with this one, Harry. So many avenues to explore."

"Perhaps I'd better get a night's rest. Big day tomorrow." I got up to leave. "Oh, by the way, I saw Tom Williams earlier. Fox is going to cop a plea and CPS have agreed not to oppose a lighter sentence. But Tom's still pressuring him to cough on his associates and give him time served."

"Fingers crossed. Too much stuff coming in via the marinas."

"Well, goodnight, Ray. Must do this again soon."

"Bring Poll next time."

I gave Ray the middle finger and we both laughed.

Outside was definitely on the chilly side and I buttoned my coat and turned the collar up. I decided to drive after all and walked back to the station to collect my car. Instead of driving straight home I headed out east of the town centre and drove down a couple streets favoured by streetwalkers, a short distance from the rail station for those who commuted in. It was quiet and a couple I did see were huddled together sharing a cigarette. Their heads came up as I drove past then down again when I didn't slow down. A bit late for business but their pimp would keep them out on the off-chance. This wasn't the place for my girl or her killer.

I was too late for the Chippy, so no supper for me this night. I made a pot of tea and checked my emails. Nothing good: spam, adult dating invitations (unsolicited). I did some searches for the local scene that might yield clues about Mariana but my lack of skill at picking search terms did not help. Deciding I'd check with Phil Harding first thing in the morning, I hit the sack.

Morning came early for me. Still dark so I needed to see the LED clock to tell me it was 4.50. I tried to get back to sleep but failed. I got up, shivering as the central heating hadn't come on so I hit the override and made a pot of coffee while the flat warmed up and I could take a shower. Breakfast TV had nothing on our murder other than a brief mention of a body of a young woman found in a flat. I expected a bigger interest from the Press later as details were released. The shower perked me up and I easily resisted switching to cold to finish. I tried that once as a kid, at my dad's suggestion it would toughen me up, and it was bloody awful.

Early at the station but the canteen didn't keep hours so I ordered a hearty breakfast to see me through the day. The vending machine delivered two Mars bars – I could replace Andy's and keep one as emergency supplies. I filled the reservoir on the coffee maker with fresh water and took the dirty mugs to clean. Until my brain woke up I was no good for solving crime so domestic distraction passed the time and, a benefit, my team could start work immediately when they got in and not have to do these tasks (seen as the most important ones). Eventually, I couldn't wait for Polly to get in so I took a filter and filled the requisite amount of ground coffee to make a jug and switched the machine on. Polly didn't get the role of coffee-maker as a sexist decision – she was the most competent and conscientious about stocking supplies and volunteered. The smell of coffee was a stimulant until I could chug some down. I think I had increased my coffee/caffeine intake incrementally since the last cigarette.

Polly was the first to arrive and, through my open door, I could see her stop in amazement by the coffee machine. She looked round and I raised my cup to her in salute. She walked over.

"That's a first."

"No, it was a thirst."

Polly looked over her shoulder to check no one else had arrived before she spoke.

"I did what you asked. It was about thirty minutes before all the pressure marks of my bra had gone. But we don't know if the process continues after death. Perhaps the pathologist would know. My next door neighbour does nude work for art classes and photographers. I asked her and she said models were advised to wear loose clothing on way to sessions so no time was lost in the studio. I think it's a dead end, boss."

"Yeah, I agree. A wild chance. Thanks for doing it anyway."

"Anything come in overnight?"

"I had a beer with Ray Axel last night, he sends his regards. Nothing unusual on the streets. No new players in town. The kids still come down from London to sell. We need to find out how she advertised her services and, particularly, what those services were. Get Harding on to it as soon as he comes in. Check for a website and social media."

"No computer in the flat. She must have done everything on her smart phone."

"It would help if we could find it. I've got a thought."

I contacted the holding unit for Martin Fox, the boyfriend.

"We need to know the contacts on his phone. Especially one Mariana Gosling. Get back to me asap."

Polly laughed. " A Fox and a Gosling together. Who'd have thought."

"If we're lucky, he'll have her number and we can work from there."

My phone rang.

"Morgan. Oh, hi. That's quick. Thank you." I wrote down the number they gave me and passed it to Polly.

"Give this to Harding as first priority. The more we can find out the better. I want all the calls in and out, and her whereabouts over the past week, if she moved about."

"Got it." Poll took the paper and went back in the squad room, wrote it on the whiteboard. I called her back in to my office.

"I might try a call on it. Pretend to be a punter if anyone picks up. Once we have observation on it if live."

The team was arriving, picking up coffee en route to desks. Polly set up another pot of coffee. Andy came straight in my office and I filled him in on my little news.

"Early days, boss. I'll work in the office and see how much we can put on the boards. Uniform are doing a fingertip search along several routes to and from the flat to see if they can find the phone if it was ditched."

"Probably a waste of time. Our guy or girl is a cool customer. Switch off the phone, take out the simcard and battery and dispose of at leisure later. Hoping for historical information from her service provider."

"We'll let the guys do it anyway. Might encourage the public to approach."

"OK, Andy. Let's get to it."

My phone rang. It was Alex Dawson.

"Hi, Harry. Thought you might like this bit of news. The sheet was fresh. Never been used before; all the signs of coming out of a wrapper, fold marks suggest strongly it was never used and laundered. Plus the only marks are associated with the victim, skin cells and the like."

"So our murderer brought it with him. Any clues as to manufacture or retailer?"

"No. Pretty basic, low cost. Maybe bought in a market rather than High Street, but that is just a guess on my part."

"Thanks, Alex. Everything helps at this stage. Keep me informed if any more breaks."

"Will do. Cheers." Daws hung up and my phone rang again. It was Phil Harding in the office.

"Boss. Bournemouth Echo on the line. They want a quote."

"Put them through...... Hello? Chief Inspector Morgan. How may I help you?"

"Chief Inspector. Thanks for taking my call. It's the murder in Boscombe. We're preparing the afternoon edition. Is there anything to add?"

"Early days. We're following several lines of enquiry."

"Can you confirm she was a prostitute?"

"We believe that may be the case but it remains to be confirmed at this stage."

"There's a rumour about Black Magic."

"No chocolate was found at the scene."

"Huh? No. *Black Magic*, as in witchcraft, devil worship."

"What we found looks like sex games. Don't go down the devil worship route for a headline. You'll look stupid later."

"Can we quote you on that?"

"Ask the Press Office for a release. That will contain all the information we can share at the moment. The victim's family have yet to be contacted and informed so let's be sensitive about what is printable. I'll let you know if we make a breakthrough."

"OK. Thanks."

Damn. Idle talk somewhere. Likely to be a constable speaking without thinking. Can't put a lid on that.

"Andy!"

Andy Robins stuck his head round my door in response.

"Andy. I think we should interview Fox after all. Set it up with CPS and see if he wants a solicitor present. He's not a person of interest but he may have background to help us. Softly, softly as we don't want to bugger up his trial."

CHAPTER 6

It had all gone wrong very quickly.

The contact was supposed to be reliable but he had only gone and got himself arrested almost immediately

A message had had to be delivered that he shouldn't talk. A serious message.

That required making a signature message that could not be mistaken.

Cash at different markets for a black sheet and a big knife. The cockerel was not so easy to obtain but a source was conveniently found in Dorset – drawing attention away from home base.

So, for the sacrifice....

CHAPTER 7

Martin Fox looked dishevelled as he sat down opposite Andy and me. Something about his demeanour tickled my copper senses. Not a nice specimen of humanity. Hair long, greasy. Mean little eyes, sharp nose, bad skin.

"Martin. I'm Chief Inspector Morgan and this is Detective Sergeant Robins. We've asked to see you regarding your partner, Mariana Gosling. You are not a suspect but we're looking to fill in some details about Mariana that may help us in our investigation. Are you OK with that."

"What can I tell you? We shacked up for a while." Nasal tones gave a whiny set to his voice, whether natural or a result of snorting the white powder.

"Just tell us what Mariana was like as a person. What did she like to do? What were her favourite haunts? Did you meet her friends? That sort of thing."

Fox shifted in his chair while thinking. I felt he wasn't thinking about what he could tell us rather than what he didn't want to tell us.

"We met at a party – don't asked me where or whose, I was stoned. We started seeing each other and moved into a flat some months back. I never met any particular friends I can think of, just the general crowd we moved among."

"You are aware she was on the game." Not a question, a statement of fact as far as I was concerned.

"I know she did tricks when short of cash. I wasn't involved. You can't have me for pimping." His eyes flicked back and forth between Andy and me.

"Don't intend to, Martin. Just looking for background and ideas where to look for a killer. We believe Mariana let her killer in. So it's likely she knew the person or had no reason to fear him or her."

I could see sweat on Fox's hairline and his eyes were firmly focusing on the table as his brain worked.

"I can't think of anyone who would kill Mariana."

"Martin. Are you sure? Is there something you aren't telling us."

"I want to go back in my cell. I'm not having you trick me into anything. I have my deal with the Prosecutor."

"Martin. Mariana was killed brutally. Don't you have any feelings about that?"

"Guard! This interview is over."

I turned to Andy.

"Perhaps we should tell the Prosecution that Martin is not being helpful in a murder enquiry."

"I think we should. Anyone who won't co-operate to put a killer away doesn't deserve any deal."

"Wait! You can't take the deal back. It's nothing to do with my case. I've coughed to the drug smuggling."

"Silly not to. After all, you were caught red-handed. But you won't spill on your supplier or buyers. I think the Prosecutor will see things differently when we have a word with him."

Fox looked really scared now. The idea of a full-term prison sentence was not attractive, considering he had a record and judges don't like repeat criminals. Andy and I stood up as if leaving.

"Look. I really don't know anything. You had me nicked when Mariana died. She hadn't been in touch."

"What do you like to do in the bedroom, Martin?"

"What?"

"Straight sex? Kinky sex? Threesome?"

Fox looked at me, then Andy, then back to me.

"Doggy."

I'm guessing the black sheets et cetera were not his, on top of Alex Dawson's assessment that they were brand new.

"Never mind." Andy and I sat down again. "Did Mariana advertise on social media, classified ads?"

"I think she'd put a classified ad in the local. Offering massages. She wasn't one for technology and we didn't have a computer or broadband."

On the way out, Andy Robins spoke his thoughts.

"A bit twitchy. I get the feeling he's holding something back."

"Hard to tell. Coppers frighten him and he's been off drugs for a while. But we have one small lead. Get down the Echo office and look at back editions under Personal Services. See if we can find Marina's adverts, especially the last one."

"Will do. What's next for you?"

"Politics! Time to go back upstairs."

Andy pulled a face in sympathy which made me feel bad I was lying. I was heading home to catch up on sleep and shift a headache before it turned into a migraine. I let Andy drive off first, so that he didn't noticed which direction I was heading in.

CHAPTER 8

I'd set up the appointment, so easy. Parked my car a couple of streets away. Checked I had everything I needed in a holdall.

The cul-de-sac was quiet. I checked for uncurtained windows and faces. All clear.

I phoned up to say I was here and got the OK. I turned my phone off and removed the battery and simcard. I would not be using it again.

I had my hoodie up and I kept my head down, stooping also to disguise my height.

She answered the door, unsuspecting of what was to come. I handed over the money then passed her a black sheet to put on the bed. While she was occupied with that I was able to pour out a couple of drinks and slip the drug into her glass. After a toast and emptying the glasses, I told her to take her dressing-gown off. She was naked underneath as I had asked. I smiled. She started to smile back then the drug hit her and she slumped unconscious to the carpet.

It was easy to squat down by her and strangle her. I'd kept my fine leather gloves on all the time. She hadn't commented – she thought it was part of my fetish. I left her on the floor while I went and took back my money and collected my bag. I washed the glasses, dried them and put them away.

She was no weight at all to lift on to the bed. I took the cord from her flimsy dressing-gown and pulled it tight round her neck. There was no doubt she was already dead but the cord was both insurance and cover-up, to mess with any marks from my hands. I did a visual check of everything, running through m y mind from my arrival to this moment.

Finally, my signatures. I left the dead cockerel on the floor and stuck a knife in Mariana's chest. The polythene bag I had carried the bird in served to take her phone, which I had taken apart, removed the battery and the simcard, ensuring I left no piece behind.

Message sent.   From the Obeah

CHAPTER 9

"Harry! It's Tom Williams. Have you heard?"

The Prosecutor had phoned me on my mobile.

"Heard what, Tom?"

"Fox. We're dropping the plea acceptance and going for hard trial. A bit behind but they finally got to check his boat forensically. We got him for marijuana but the sniffer dogs got another scent and the labs tested the swabs taken of his hiding places and came up with heroin. He's carried H before."

"That explains his reaction when we went to see him about Gosling. He was hiding a dirty secret."

"Means we may have an OCG involved." [Organised Crime Group]

After the phone call ended, I filled Andy in on the news, and he asked "How were you involved in his arrest? It wasn't one of our cases."

"Sheer luck. I witnessed a traffic incident near the marina and when the boot of his car popped, saw the bags of marijuana. Called it in."

"Right place, right time, then."

"A bit of a coincidence we should find his girlfriend murdered."

"Stop her from talking? If he's in an OCG, I mean. Millions at stake."

I pulled a face. "Hmmm? Maybe. Not thinking it likely she knew much. If he was involved, she wouldn't need to pull tricks for money. I think Fox kept her in the dark."

"He might have talked in his sleep."

43

"Right. ' *I'm doing a drug run tomorrow*'. Is anyone coherent in their sleep? Isn't usually just calling out a name?"

"Don't know. Never slept with a sleeptalker."

"No. I think to be a risk as a witness and worth murdering, she'd have had to be hands on somehow. Still, we'll keep it in mind if we get nowhere with other leads."

The first days are typically slow going – the meticulous attention to detail and the collection of small bits of information to try and build on. We could always hope for a big breakthrough but it was more likely to be a hard grind. The national database had nothing similar so either this was totally new or previous escapades had not resulted in death. There was always a chance a sex game – asphyxiation kicks – gone wrong, but I felt the person would have panicked, not carried out the set dressing – that was too cold and calculated. Everyone had something to do but I felt superfluous – they didn't need me looking over their shoulders. I passed the time checking emails, filling in my expenses claim, random googling, visits to the canteen. Eventually, I went for a walk down Madeira Road and ended up at Horseshoe Common, where I plonked myself on a bench for some thinking time. We had some autumn sunshine to enjoy but I kept my coat buttoned up against the cold. My equivalent of Sherlock's three pipes would have been to have had a few cigarettes but I was still cold turkey on giving up.

Mariana Gosling – prostitute and drug user – murdered and stage dressed.

Perpetrator – unknown. Cool. Forward planner. Probably experienced in criminality but possibly never caught. Most likely Male.

Martin Fox – drug smuggler and dealer. Perfect alibi for the murder but he may have contracted. Yet I doubt he has the intelligence for what went down, more likely to pay for a simple hit. Motive – not known.

Phones! Phones! If only. Plan to check with Harding if anything.

Have we missed anything? Jumped to conclusions? No, I don't think so; we haven't rushed. Let Forensics do their stuff. Got uniform doing the streets and neighbours. Alex Dawson is the best I've known so I trust his work 100%. It still feels like we're running through treacle. I've got nothing to take to my next meeting with MacKay and she'll be blowing hot on budgets again.

Being stationary, the cold was beginning to bite, so I headed back to the nick, thinking I might have a hot pastie and a mug of tea for a change. The pigeons looked disgusted I hadn't brought food with me as I left my seat.

CHAPTER 10

A dinner invitation to Andy and Maureen's is a treat to look forward to. Maureen was an excellent cook and would try out recipes before dinner parties, so I could expect something special. I arrived at their place in Westbourne on time, with a bottle of wine and a bouquet of supermarket flowers. Andy answered the door.

"Hello, boss...Harry."

"I trust red is OK?" I said, thrusting the Australian Shiraz at him.

"Fine. Let's go through to the kitchen and find a vase for the flowers."

As we walked the hallway to the kitchen I could see into the dining room and a table laid for four. I raised an eyebrow. Andy looked embarrassed.

"I'm sorry, Harry. Mo's invited a friend from work. A woman."

"Ah!" This was disappointing. I was looking forward to a cosy evening and good grub and now I had to make polite conversation with a stranger. Worse, a female stranger, which made me think Maureen was trying matchmaking again. Maureen's voice was heard from the lounge.

"Harry! Come on in. Don't stay out there chatting with Andy."

I dutifully entered the lounge, kissed Mo on both cheeks.

"You're looking fabulous as usual." Which wasn't a lie.

"Harry, Meet Sangeeta. She's just moved into the area and is running the Personnel department at my place."

Sangeeta turned out to be an attractive Asian woman, probably mid 30s. Good clothes, not chain store I hazarded, modest amount of jewellery, and a light fragrance I didn't know.

46

"Pleased to meet you, " we said simultaneously.

Maureen jumped in. "I'll just check how dinner is doing. I'll send Andy in with drinks." and she was gone.

I spoke first. "Dorset. What attracted you?"

"Good train service to London. Cheaper houses. And promotion to head of Personnel."

"Any family here?"

"No. But I think I'll make friends. Maureen and Andy seem nice and Maureen has helped me settle in at work."

"Yes, They're a lovely couple."

"Andy is your sergeant, right?"

"I don't own him. But, yes, Andy is on my team."

"Your job must be fascinating."

"Not really. Occasional moments of drama followed by days and weeks of boring graft. Excuse me, I'll see what is holding up the drinks."

I really wanted to have a relaxing evening and be fed some good grub, better than the Takeaway or the Instant meal I would have had at my flat, so I was probably a bit abrupt when I stepped into the kitchen and caught Andy and Maureen having words in quiet.

"Harry!" Andy spoke first."The drinks! I'll be right there."

"Maureen." I said, with a look.

"Harry. Just chat. Sangeeta doesn't know anyone here so I invited her for company..like Andy does for you." That was me admonished and a little less bristly Harry Morgan returned to the lounge.

"Drinks coming along soon. Sorry. Been a hard day."

"Maureen did say you and Andy were investigating a murder. That can't be nice. I can't imagine you ever get used to it."

47

"We learn to be professional. No good to be emotive, gets in the way of a clear mind to find and collect evidence."

"Is it that easy?"

"No. It's not easy at all. When it's all over, we tend to go on a bender to find release. As long as we get our man or woman. Unfortunately, we're the late emergency service, we don't prevent, we punish."

At the moment, Andy came in with a tray of drinks, followed by Maureen who spoke.

"Not long now. Hope you've got an appetite."

"Starving, Mo. Smells good." A compliment and a truth. I hadn't eaten since breakfast, skipped the canteen pasty at lunchtime, in order to make room for Maureen's cooking, as Andy had headed me off with the invite. How Andy did not balloon on such fare, I don't know. Maybe he's blessed with a calorie destroying metabolism.

With aperitivos, Maureen served up bruschetta – toasted bread pieces with warm tomato, a drizzle of extra virgin oil and basil, with black and green olives. A choice for main course was meatballs in spaghetti with tomato sauce or lasagne, rich and creamy. Maureen made both pastas from scratch. Dessert was tiramisu or cheesecake; I had some of both.

The evening passed well enough. No one talked shop, just about how nice it was to live in this part of the country. Where to visit around town, which were the best cafes, how busy the town got in summer with the holidaymakers. When it was time to depart, Andy phoned for a taxi for Sangeeta and I to share. Sangeeta lived nearer so the driver was told to go to her address first.

The taxi pulled up outside Sangeeta's house in Branksome. She was renting a modest two-bed property while she looked for somewhere to buy, she had told me during dinner.

"Well, goodnight, Harry. It was nice to meet you."

"Yes, same here."

"You know. Maureen has my phone number if you fancy meeting for a drink sometime. Help a stranger in town."

"Well. Work. Awkward hours. Can't promise. Busy time right now. Wouldn't wait to book something then let you down at the last minute. "

"I see. No problem. Forget I asked."

"Goodnight."

Sangeeta got out of the taxi and I waited to see her go indoors before I told the driver to take me home.

"You know, mate, that's a classy bird you've just kissed off."

"Didn't ask for your opinion; don't want it. If you want a tip, no more conversation."

Right then, my mobile phone rang. I didn't recognise the number but when I heard what the caller had to say I gave new instructions to the taxi driver.

"Change of plan. Take me to A&E Poole."

"You feeling alright?"

"Yeah. I'm not going to die in your cab. Can you get a move on? If you get pulled over I'll deal with it. I'm a cop."

I think the taxi driver was rather excited to get permission to burn rubber as we arrived outside the hospital within minutes. The fare was just under 15 but I threw a twenty at him with "Keep the change."

Inside A&E it was moderately busy, being too early for pub chuck out and later than most people worked. I saw a uniformed constable standing outside a cubicle.

"I'm Chief Inspector Morgan. Did you get the call to me?"

"Yes, sir. In here."

He led me into the cubicle, where a 70 year old male was receiving treatment to cuts on his face.

"Hello, Harry. What you doing here?"

"Hello, dad. Got a call about a fracas at the Butcher's Arms. Description sounded like you."

"No problem. A couple of punks got stroppy with Dave as he wouldn't serve them. We threw them out."

The police constable spoke up. "Threw them out and called an ambulance. They're getting patched up in the next room. They want to bring charges."

I went into the next examination room where two twenty something males were being treated for cuts and bruises, getting stitched, looking far worse than my dad, and flashed my warrant card, doing it quickly so they couldn't see my name.

"I hear you want to press charges for assault."

"We fucking well do."

"OK. Constable take down the details. Two young men have their arses kicked by two pensioners. Write it up properly and I'll attend to the press release."

"Wait! What?"

"That's what happened isn't it? You went in the Butchers and had a fight with a seventy year old and a sixty year old. They threw you into the street. The Echo will want to report it so we'll need to prepare a press release."

I thought it pertinent to omit to mention that my dad and his mate Dave were ex-Royal Marines.

The two men looked at each other and reached an agreement. "Perhaps we won't bother with charges. Nothing much happened. We'll forget it."

"If you're sure."

"Just a misunderstanding."

I nodded, acting reluctant, then left them. Dave arrived at that moment, having been parking his car.

"Hello, Harry. Long time no see."

"Hi, Dave. He's in there. Won't be long. Keep away from those two punks though. You've done enough damage. They've seen the error of their ways."

"Thanks, Harry. Come by for a drink soon. We'd like to see you."

"If I can find the time, Dave. You go careful now. See you around."

It was my father who had given me the mantra - "*It's a good day when everybody gets to go home.*"

I decided to walk to my flat, it wasn't that far on a lovely evening and I'd burn some calories off, having overeaten by an extra portion of dessert that was irresistible.

CHAPTER 11

The two punks had been doing a pub crawl but they didn't know the area. The Butcher's Arms had a specialist clientele. I was working the bar as usual when they came in. They looked like trouble from the start – loud and coarse. We weren't busy but Frank was practising on the pool table and although he never showed any interest his body language changed.

The punks came up to the bar.

"Two pints of lager and vodka chasers."

Not even a please and slurring his words.

"Not tonight, lads. You look like you've enjoying yourselves too much already. Why not head home and get some kip?"

"Fuck off, old man. You gonna get us our drinks or what? We're the fucking customers here."

"Bars closed to non-regulars, guys. We're having a club night. Let's do this nicely. Move on."

"You fucking wanker! Don't tell us to move on."

"Easy lads. No need for this. Bars closed to you. Just turn round and leave."

Their mistake was they didn't. Instead, one reached over the counter to try and grab my shirt. I grabbed his hand and pulled him forward.

"Enough! Go while you can. No one wants trouble, boys."

Apparently his mate wanted trouble and tried to leap the bar. He succeeded in knocking me back but before he could land on my side of the counter, Frank had pulled him back.

"Alright, Dave, I've got this one."

I let go of the first one and came round the bar. They were pumped with alcohol and thought two old guys were easy meat..... wrong.

CHAPTER 12

The next morning saw some of us off the murder case for a while. The priority was to find a missing 5 year old girl. I led a briefing at the station

"Alright. Quiet down. For those from another nick who don't know me, I'm Detective Chief Inspector Harry Morgan. This lady is Detective Sergeant Polanski, aka Polly when you get to know her. Now, last night, a young girl went missing from her home."

Polly took over: "Laura Jenkins, five years old. Her mother put her to bed by eight o'clock. Just after nine, the mother went to the newsagents, two streets away, to buy cigarettes. When she got back, she looked in on Laura and her bed was empty. She checked round the house then went to a neighbour who phoned it in."

We tag-teamed the briefing. "A patrol car answered and checked the house and garden then called it in to CID. They said the mother, Ellen Jenkins, was less than coherent, looked the worse for wear and the bin had empty vodka bottles. She said she needed cigarettes, couldn't find her keys and left the front door unlocked. CCTV footage from the newsagents shows her in the shop at nine twenty five. The walk to the shop takes around five minutes max. So that's ten minutes walking and maybe another five shopping. So a window of fifteen minutes for Laura to go missing."

"We had officers checking the neighbourhood last night and first thing this morning we have teams knocking on doors, asking if esidents have seen anything and to check outbuildings and garages."

"We all know time is critical for a missing child. We are considering he various options. One. Laura woke, couldn't find her mother and vent looking for her. The media will be full of her photo this morning asking people to be alert. She's very noticeable, a lovely girl, long blonde hair, blue eyes and will be in pyjamas.

Two. She was abducted. If from the home, then it was planned. If picked up on the street, it was opportunistic. We have a team checking on all known and suspected sex offenders in the district."

A face I didn't recognise spoke up. "DC Dave Wilkins. What about her father? A lot of abductions are family matters."

I'd done some homework before the briefing. "Not living with them and supposed to be serving in Germany with the Army. That needs checking. Now option three. She's not been abducted. She didn't go missing last night. So I've asked for a cadaver dog. At best it eliminates one possibility. At worst, we find out what did happen.

That got some gasps.

Polly stepped in. "The boss and I are going to Laura's school next. We'll check when she last attended, whether staff noticed any change of behaviour and we'll pick up the Visitors Log for follow up on who may have seen her at school."

Time to get the squad on the road.

"You've been assigned tasks. Team A are to collect CCTV from the neighbourhood. It's a poor district so not many private cameras, maybe a few motorists have one. Check road cameras. Run plates through the system and cross-reference names with known offenders.

Team B to go over the home for clues and interview closest neighbours. I'll take anything, even gossip, at this moment. Clock is ticking. Go to it. Team leaders meet back here at noon to report."

Midday came round and we assembled in the station again for updates.

"Everyone here? Right. Polly. You go first."

"School visit revealed nothing. Laura is a happy child, has friends. We've been given a copy of the Visitors Log to be checked back for two weeks to start with. "

Dave Wilkins had something to contribute: "Boss. I followed up on the father. He doesn't live with the mother anymore and MoD confirm he is in Germany on exercises. I've also checked on the mother, and she's been arrested for possession and shoplifting in the past. Cautions both times."

"Thanks, Dave. It all helps to paint a picture of the family environment. Less likely this is a family abduction now. Cadaver dog is due this afternoon but let's focus on Laura being alive and kept somewhere or she's got herself into a situation she can't get out of, maybe looked for shelter and got locked in. "

Polly added, "Nothing from the neighbourhood team but they are still at it. Supervised volunteers are joining in the search."

I looked round the room. All faces carrying a hint of worry and also an eagerness to get back out there. We wouldn't find Laura in the station.

"I'll be live on the lunchtime news appealing for witnesses. Not asking the mother to attend – we're saying she is too upset and is under medical supervision. I'd better get out to the Press now and prepare. Polly. Take over here, please, and fill me in when I get back. We'll take a drive over to see the house again."

The Press interview was done quickly. I came back indoors to find Polly waiting to drive me. We got in the car and headed out before speaking.

"How did the Press thing go?"

"Fine, I think. I gave a statement and took a couple of questions. They'll want more for the evening news. Turn right here."

"The dog? Think there's a chance Laura is dead?"

"I hope not. But we have to eliminate that possibility. There may have been an accident and the mother covering up. Or she may have flipped when drunk, got heavy-handed.... Nobody is to say we're looking for a body. The story is we're looking for a scent trail."

"Shouldn't we be doing that anyway?"

I patted my pocket for cigarettes, in a moment of distraction.

"I checked with the Canine Unit. There was rain after midnight that would have washed any trail away."

Polly barely beat a traffic light change to red. In an unmarked car, we got glares from a couple of drivers, but Polly was unfazed and continued the conversation.

"I wish we could get more sense out of the mother. We don't know what type of nightwear Laura was wearing, just pyjamas, and if she wore slippers. "

I had a thought. "Let's find out if they are known to Social Services. If they had a Social Worker visiting, she may remember something."

57

"Or 'he' may remember something."

"I've never met a male social worker. That would be a first. Stop here. I need to get some lunch and I'd like to question the newsagent.
"

Polly pulled up kerbside and put the hazard flashers on and I jumped out. I heard her phone ring and she answered, "Polanski."

"It's Dave Wilkins here. Is the boss with you?"

"Yes, but not right this second. What you got?"

"A teddy bear was found in the next street. I'll ping a photo over. See if Laura had a teddy like this one."

"Will do. " Polly's phone pinged; I heard it as I returned to the car. "Got it.... Let uniform have a pic as well. This is likely just a pram drop from a parent taking a child out. When they do doorknocks on that street, they can ask."

I could hear Wilkins as I climbed in the car.

"Roger that. See you later."

"Yeah, bye.

"Cold sausage rolls, I'm afraid."

"Not for me, thanks. Here, look at my phone....we need to see if it can be identified as Laura's. Found a street away from her home.

"OK. Let the Family Liaison unit have it. Whoever is babysitting the mother can ask her. Let's get to the house. I want to be there when the dog is working."

The house was a small mid-terrace affair, nothing exciting. This wasn't a postcode area with money. Inside I asked, "Which is Laura's bedroom?"

Polly knew "On the left." and led the way. The room needed decorating, actually it needed a bloody good clean first.

"God! Not much here. Mattress on the floor, not a proper bed."

"Can't judge. Single parent, not much money." Polly seemed less shocked than I was.

"Enough for vodka."

"Cheapest brands. May be shoplifted."

I took the scene in. "There's a rabbit. How many soft toys might a child have?"

"Usually more than one but the rabbit being on the mattress suggests this is her favourite. Makes the teddy less likely to be hers."

"But not impossible. Don't rule it out yet but don't let it distract us. Was the street where it was found the way to the shops or Laura's school?"

Polly thought. "Hmmm. Shops I think. School the other way."

"Laura might think 'shops' if she's looking for her mum."

"Down to habits. Did mum go to the shops often and not so much to a neighbour?"

I clenched and unclenched my fists. "This is frustrating, Polly. There's a five year old out there depending on us and we're going round in circles."

Polly was looking through the window into the back yard. "I can see the dog checking the garden. Come over to the window."

I joined her and watched the cadaver dog and its handler working, "I hope it finds nothing."

"Me too."

Rather than stand staring, and not wanting to be watching if the dog made a discovery, I proposed "Let's look in the mother's room."

The mother had the other bedroom, one at the front, overlooking the street. "Not as messy as I expected. Take a look in the wardrobe."

Polly opened the wardrobe door. "What are we looking for?"

"Anything. Anything that might give us a clue." Hoping and keeping busy.

Polly pushed the clothes on the rack and took a look at the floor of the robe. "Nothing exceptional. Cheap clothing, charity shops purchases possibly. No menswear. "

I'd been opening drawers in a bedside chest. "Nothing here. No drugs or anything that would be out of place for a single woman.... Polly.... Is there anything we're not doing that we should be?"

Polly gave me a straight look, "You've organised everyone. It takes time."

"Time is what we haven't got. Let's go for a walk. Get some fresh air and let's absorb the neighbourhood for inspiration. I can't bear inactivity."

Outside was autumn fresh in a dingy street. Litter in the gutter, dog mess on the pavement. The Dog Unit was placing the alsatian back in the van, shaking his head at us.

I spoke my thoughts out loud. "A five year old would not be walking these streets alone. Do you think she did? Not just last night but any time?"

"Unlikely. You don't send a five year old on errands. She would have walked it with her mother, know the route. There's Dave Wilkins ahead. DAVE! ..."

Polly's shout got his attention and he hurried towards us.

"Oh, hi. Teddy bear seems a dead end. Took a look at it myself and it was bone dry. Could not have been dropped last night. Some kiddy lost it this morning."

At least we weren't wasting time on a false lead. "Never mind. It needed checking. "

Wilkins looked disappointed though. "What we got so far?"

Polly answered. "Nothing. Canine said the dog found nothing, so good news but not a clue as to where she is."

Wilkins looked a bit worn down by the lack of progress. "Uniforms coming up dead ends. House calls nothing. Searches zilch."

Something caught my eye. "What's that?"

Wilkins looked in the same direction as I was indicating but couldn't see what was attracting my attention. "What?"

I pointed. "On that telly. Look through the window."

Polly checked it. "Kids TV. I think that's Paw Patrol."

"But aren't these retirement flats? Plus kids aren't out of school yet."

"What you thinking, boss?"

"Not sure. But I'd like to knock on that door....."

We walked across the road together. I worked out which was the door to the ground floor flat with the TV on. We rang the bell and waited for the door to be answered. A small, elderly woman eventually opened it.

"Yes? Sorry I'm Catholic, don't need Jehovah's Witnesses."

Polly stepped forward, being less intimidating than two males.

"We're police officers. May we know your name."

"Police, Oh, dear. I'm Mrs O'Brien."

I put on a gentle tone of voice. "Is there a Mr O'Brien?"

Mrs O'Brien took a pause before answering. "No, dear. My husband passed away many years ago. I'm all on my own. "

Polly did some empathising. "You must get lonely."

Mrs O'Brien perked a bit. "I have Charles for company."

"Charles?" I asked

"My cat," she explained.

I felt Mrs O'B was a little out of it, not dementia perhaps, but needed handling carefully.

"I like cats... Mrs O'Brien. Could I have a glass of water, I'm rather dry."

"Of course. Do come in.........." and she stepped aside to let us enter.

Polly was the first to notice. "Harry. In the lounge. "

I joined her in the doorway. "Mrs O'Brien?"

Mrs O'B beamed. "This is my young friend. I was calling Charles in last night and she was walking down the road, crying. I brought her in and made her a hot chocolate and a biscuit. She was exhausted, poor thing. She fell asleep on the sofa. We've been watching cartoons all day. "

Polly started back into police mode. "Mrs O'Brien. This is Laura Jenkins. She's been missing from home since last night."

The old lady looked genuinely surprised. "Has she, dear? She's been very happy here. We've been watching TV together."

I'd gone over to the sofa and had tried shaking Laura gently, to rouse her. "Why won't she wake up?"

"I gave her one of my sleeping tablets in her morning milk. She kept asking to go home but I didn't know where she lived. She's been lovely company."

62

I could feel a pulse but I was worried about how far Laura was out and whether she'd been overdosed with sedatives. "Polly. Phone for an ambulance. We need her checked over. Mrs O'Brien, will you go with this officer into the kitchen and make us all a cup of tea. Dave."

"This way, my love. I'll give you a hand." Wilkins gently guided her from the room.

We had the team assembled for the debrief. I called for silence.

"OK. Quiet down...... A good result. Laura is safe. No side effects from the sleeping tablet. We won't be charging Mrs O'Brien but Social Services will be dealing with her. "

Dave Wilkins spoke. "And the mother?"

I let Polly answer. "Social Services will do an assessment. The School is getting involved too. They have a Welfare Fund and also a Parents Group for support. "

At least the day had finished better than it had started.

A good day when everybody gets to go home

"So, good work everyone. Down the pub. First round on me." Which got a cheer."Down at the Butchers; I get a discount there."

CHAPTER 13

The Butcher's Arms was its usual busy self. My father was playing darts
noisily with some others that looked ex-military. The pub was broad
church for the Armed Services and ex-Army met ex-Navy with friendly
rivalry at the dartboard and pool table but joined ranks against outsiders.
Dolly Parton was singing her heart out on the jukebox. Country & Western
sat side by side with Heavy Metal – Dave was a Black Sabbath hardcore
fan. It had an old-fashioned feel to the place, like it didn't belong in the
21st century and the only authentic things missing was a fug from cigarette
smoke. The pool table hadn't long replaced a bar billiards table. Two
dartboards at the end of parallel tracks from two oches. The only
concession to modern today was a large screen tv on a wall. The long bar
had a choice of ales and lagers, this being a Free House owned by Dave.
If you were hungry there were pork scratchings, crisps and nuts. Dave had
no issues about regulars bringing in kebabs from the Turkish caterer down
the road.

I had sat with Polly at a corner table with a good view of everything.
Polly leaned in to me, a vodka and tonic clutched in her hand."Is that
really your dad?"

"What it says on my birth certificate." I took a sip of my Fursty Ferret, a
Blandford beer,

"Did you have a good relationship growing up?"

"He was away a lot. That's being in the services. But when he was home, yes, he was a good father. Never raised a hand or his voice to my mother or me."

"Where I am from, it's cultural to keep women and kids in line with a slap or worse."

"Same here a couple of generations back. Times change but not always behind closed doors. No, I can't complain. When he was home, he'd take me camping, teach me survival skills. I think he thought he was preparing me to to be in the Marines like him."

"Why didn't you?"

"Not keen on being sent overseas to kill people." That created a few moments of silence, before I continued. "When I was ten or eleven, I asked him 'how many people have you killed?' It seemed thrilling that my dad was some sort of hero like in my comics and in the movies. I'll never forget his look. 'We don't keep count and we don't tell. It's not something to take pride in' he said."

"Was he disappointed when you chose the police?"

"I suspect he was, at first. But he never said anything and maybe he is OK with me doing something in service and not being a capitalist."

Dave came over with drinks for us, casting an eye at Polly and then me.

"From Frank and me. You coming back to watch the match on Saturday?"

"Not into football, Dave. Cricket man."

"Not the beautiful game though is it?"

"It is for me. I think it's the only game that is both a team sport and a solo sport."

Dave didn't get it, so I explained.

65

"Think about it. One on one – bowler to batsman. At that time the batsman is on his own. The bowler would like a clean wicket take or lbw. Failing that he hopes to make the batsman make a mistake and his team members will catch or stump out. The batsman has total single responsibility for surviving and then scoring. Best moment ever – Ben Stokes in the World Cup Final."

"I'll give you that." Dave moved on.

Polly spoke. "I didn't have you down for any sports."

"Was at school. Decent enough at the wicket, terrible bowler. No time to watch sport now."

Polly nodded in the direction of Frank and Dave.

"They both look like they've been in a fight."

"Don't ask."

Andy Robins was giving Phil Harding a thrashing at pool. Although they had stayed on the Mariana Gosling murder and not participated in the missing child enquiry, I had phoned them to come on over and have a drink.

"Andy. Can you and Phil come in early tomorrow? I need to catch up."

"No problem. Seven OK?"

"Great. I'll have the coffee on. " I stood up. "There's another round behind the bar, but I'm getting going. See you all in the morning."

"Night, boss."

"Going so soon, Harry?"

"Yes. Want a clear head and I rather fancy an early night. Well done again on Laura. Everyone did their bit and we got her home."

As promised, Andy and Phil Harding arrived at 7, Andy carrying warm bacon rolls, mustard and ketchup, for us.

As we ate, they brought me up to speed. I had been in at 6 and perused the boards as well as getting the coffee-machine going, but it was good to hear from them.

"CCTV is a bust at the moment. Too big a net to cast."

Harding added, "The immediate neighbourhood is low income so no one is spending on home security tech. As we move more and more streets away, we increase the square yardage exponentially so too many houses or car owners to canvass."

Andy continued, "That takes us to commercial CCTV and public systems. Just too much material to go through. Busy streets. We need to narrow down the times if we can."

I rubbed my chin. "OK. Put that on the back burner. If we get a tighter timeframe or, better still, some indication of route for the murderer, we'll put resources on it. We need suspects. People we can investigate and see how they match up."

Polly arrived, gave us a dirty look for the empty but unclean coffee jug. I made an apologetic shrug and she reached over and took my hardly started second cup for herself.

The four of us sat at a table.

"We've a serious lack of evidence. The murder scene was clean. Her phone is missing. No witnesses to any before or after activity. I've got pressure from upstairs about budgets because 'it's only a prossie'. Damn. Yorkshire started with 'it's only a prossie', same with Ipswich."

"Boss. Do you think we might have a serial killer then?"

"Too early to say. Gut says we have something else but I can't figure what. Sutcliffe and Wright were messy killers, no scene setting. Our guy c girl went into the victim's home, was let in, and took their time. Is fetish the buzz or misdirection? If we could find the phone...."

Harding spoke. "If only. Criminals are unaware about how much can be gathered from their mobiles. If I were to commit a crime, I'd get a burner and immediately destroy after. Dismantle, pour lighter fuel over it and ligh' it up. Then throw it in a river after."

"That's a professional approach. The amateur holds on to things. The phone might still be out there."

"At least you were able to get her number, boss. Info is it went offline the night she was murdered and hasn't been switched on since. We're getting the locations data to see where she moved around. I'll make up a streetmap when I get that."

"Thanks, Phil. We can retrace her steps and show photos to see if anyone has a memory of her and especially anyone she was with."

While we were talking, a phone had rung in the office and Polly had answered it and taken a message, which she now related to us. "That wa: Alex Dawson. Early tox tests indicate rohypnol. Explains her compliance and no struggle."

"Again. Premeditated."

"The knife. Hers or brought in?"

"Brought in, boss. She has a cheap knife set, none missing from the rack and not similar one to the murder weapon. That suggests the murderer had not been in the flat before and brought a weapon with him i case none available on site."

"So it is pointing to a planned kill, not a fetish game gone wrong. Phil. I want to hear if anything has come up on National Database for similar. I know we've already had a go, but vary the search terms, widen it a bit. The black cockerel might be a new feature as the killer develops his modus operandi."

"On it, boss."

Polly had answered a second phone call. "Boss. We've got a woman and her solicitor down at front desk. Says she wants to talk to the man in charge of the Mariana Gosling case."

Andy and I exchanged looks; neither of us had an idea about what this might mean but keen to find out.

"OK, get them brought up to an interview room, Poll. I want you in the room with me. Andy. You watch on the monitor."

The solicitor was Henry Goodfellow. We hadn't crossed paths before so introductions were made. A thin fellow in a double-breasted pinstripe suit, a bit shiny at the elbows, pale blue shirt and pink tie. He explained why they were here.

"My client is a friend of Miss Gosling and thinks she may have some information. What she would like is an assurance you won't charge her if, during her statement, she reveals possible criminal activity."

I looked at his client. About the same age as Mariana, I guessed. Bottle-blonde, contact lenses to make her eyes blue, and cheekbones sharp enough to slice salami and enough cleavage showing to give you vertigo.

"I can't make any such promise, not knowing what criminal activity might be revealed. What I can promise is, should it appear that your client is withholding evidence and not assisting our investigation, I will charge her with the obstruction of justice then investigate her until I know her great grandmother's name, date of birth, everyone in between and what brand of coffee your client drinks." Then I decided to become the Good Cop.

"But I am not interested in any petty offences, recreational drug use, prostitution at this time. I have a murderer to catch and he, or she, is out there and may kill again. Can we proceed?"

Goodfellow and the woman exchanged glances and she gave a small nod. Goodfellow spoke, "I will interrupt if I think my client is being unwise and I would like some time with her to discuss how to continue."

"Understood. Right, miss, can we have your name, address and date of birth for the record. My sergeant is going to take notes."

The woman was called Jazmine Strong.

"I've known Mariana for some time. Met her on a porn shoot. There's this guy who makes wankfilms for the internet. Nothing too heavy, just wiggling and flash our bits, pretend a bit of girl-on-girl action. One hundred each for an afternoon's work."

"Ever anything a bit kinky?"

"What? Like spanking or bondage?"

"Anything a bit more fetish than girls together."

"We do pretend spanking but neither of us like pain so that's a market for those who can take a bit. Just nice undies, black stuff is preferred, stockings, that sort of thing."

"Can we have the name of the producer? He's not in trouble but he may know more."

Jazmine obliged. "I liked Mariana. She was good people. We only do this sort of stuff to make ends meet. "

"Do you know her drug dealer?"

"I don't do drugs."

"Not saying you do, Jazmine, but Mariana did and it's another lead for us."

"Yeah, OK. It was her skanky boyfriend, Martin Fox."

Polly and I exchanged looks. Dead end there, we both thought.

I continued with the questioning but Jazmine had nothing specific to add, so I asked if we could look at her phone to see any messages between her and Mariana. That was when Goodfellow placed his hand on Jazmine's arm and turned to me.

"I can't ask my client to do that, Inspector. As she is not suspected of any crime you can't make her hand her phone over."

"How about you look at it and write down the times and dates of all calls between them? And, if there is anything else that is not incriminating but may help our enquiries will you write that down for us. This is a nasty murder and the killer is out there."

Goodfellow only took a second before he nodded to Jazmine and took out a fountain pen. Polly pushed a pad over to him.

I spoke again. "We'll leave you to it. Can I have coffee or tea sent in?"

Both declined, keen to get this over and get out, I suppose.

"When you have finished with your solicitor, I'll have an officer take you home."

"I can't have no copper pulling up at my pad."

"Don't worry. He'll be plainclothes in an unmarked car."

71

We left them to it but I told Harry to keep viewing the monitor and listen in. In the office I called Harding in.

"Lose that tie and undo a couple of top buttons. Polly. Mess his hair up a bit. Phil, I need you to take this woman back to her place away from her brief and get a look at her computer and videocamera. Make copies of anything you think will help us, especially if you recognise Mariana's flat in the video. We can compare old pictures with how we saw it. Be subtle about how you get her to allow it. Suggest she might be vulnerable and you'd be happy to check for viruses."

Harding was quick on the uptake. "I'll take a memory stick with me."

"Good man."

It's like doing a jigsaw. You know you don't have all the pieces, they arrive bit by bit, and there is no box with a cover photo, so you take what you do know and apply that to sorting out the bits you do have. Eventually the hope is you can see what is appearing and the gaps don't matter because you have enough to understand what the whole picture is going to be.

CHAPTER 14

When word reaches you that you're a person of interest to the law and no longer anonymous, it's time to upsticks and go on holiday.

Mariana and Jazmine had been good workers. Inexpensive and able to put on a show.
I'd had requests for "snuff" films and we'd started off with a few fakes and I got offered a lot of money for more detail. Sometimes one can be too much of a professional. If the cops were watching my videos......

I had already moved all my kit to a lock-up under a fake name. Handwritten out all my phone contacts then destroyed my phone.

The sooner I caught Ryan Air from Hurn, the better.

CHAPTER 15

I called the team together for a catch up. Once they were settled and paying attention, I began.

"It might seen we are not making progress at the moment, but everything we are doing could provide the one breakthrough to crack this case open. We have some new information on Mariana just in this morning. Phil Harding is following that up as I speak. He's making progress on the tracking of the victim's phone prior to the murder and will put than on our database, so you'll be able to log in and compare dates, times and places with your paths of investigation to see if any intersect. Where the data shows Mariana at a business, we'll go there and take any CCTV footage to see if she was alone or whether anyone was paying attention to her. Andy."

Andy took over. "We are almost one hundred percent certain the cockerel at the flat is the one taken from the Dorchester farmer. At the time the theft was reported, there was an illegal Travellers' camp and the local force assumed it was taken for the pot, so didn't follow up. We now have them taking all access roads to the farm and knocking on doors to ask if anyone has home security filming or saw anything unusual, particularly a vehicle they did not recognise as local. Anything that comes up may help us when we go back to our own CCTV collection around the flat."

My turn again.

"The killer was very careful. Nothing picked up from the flat and any DNA samples are not on the system. A very cool customer. He, and I say he because that is how I feel it, but don't ignore women just yet, premeditated the murder by obtaining a cockerel, a knife and rohipnol. It's looking possible he visited the flat or the vicinity beforehand but only once, so as to know the layout, maybe a practice run, and to be certain that Mariana did not have a partner there. Polly."

Polly checked her notes.

"The victim was a sex worker. She didn't pull in from the street and she made titillation movies for the internet, partnered with another woman, who gave us a statement this morning. We'll be tracking down the agent who ordered the movies and uploaded them. He is a Person of Interest until proved otherwise. When he's back, Harding will be working with a small team on the tech stuff – finding her social media and how she might have attracted clients on line. There are fetish websites where services are advertised. Or someone may have seen a movie of her, identified her and made contact. There will be traces if we look in the right places."

"The motive is unclear. No sign of sexual activity by the killer or the victim, just visual. Maybe a voyeur, unable to perform. Maybe he, or she, takes photos and self-pleasures when back in their home. Maybe a Snuff movie. Another job for Harding's team is to check the National Database for similar crimes, not all ending in murder. Use points of similarity to make matches. Try searching by mixing the search terms around for a broad reveal. This afternoon, I am filming an appeal that will go out this evening on BBC South and ITV Meridian. I will mention some items we've kept quiet about so be ready for the phones to ring with a few nutcases. I suggest you take breaks now, get something to eat and be here this evening to field phone calls. Any questions?"

Alison raised her hand to get my attention.

"Yes, Alison."

"I take it we haven't found the phone?"

"Correct. And it's unlikely we will, at least in a condition to help us. The phone stopped at the time of the murder. The killer would have taken out the simcard and battery while in the flat and probably has destroyed or effectively dumped all the pieces. But we can hope to find it in his or her possession when we make an arrest, and we will, as another fat tick for prosecution.

I sat with Andy and Polly in my office and watched the early evening news with my appeal. The crew were in the outer office, ready to take calls.

"We're investigating the brutal murder of Mariana Gosling (*photo up on screen*) three nights ago. Mariana was strangled then a knife pushed into her chest (*photo of knife*). If you sold such a knife recently or know someone who bought a knife like this, we'd like to talk to them.

An unusual feature at the crime scene was that the killer left a decapitated black cockerel. We believe the cockerel was taken from Forrets Farm near Dorchester recently (*map up showing location*) so, again, if you know someone who had a black cockerel in their possession recently we'd like to talk to them. Or, if that was you, please contact us so we may eliminate you from the murder enquiry. If any of what I have said is ringing bells with you we'd rather you called us than just think 'No, I'm not sure'. Let us decide what is relevant or not. Use the phone number at the bottom of the screen to make a confidential call to one of our officers. All calls will be treated with respect. Finally. Mariana was a sex worker. If you were a client, let me assure you, you have nothing to fear from the investigation. If you come forward we will keep your details confidential and it will help to eliminate you from our enquiries early on and you may be able to help paint a picture for us of who Mariana was. Mariana was a young woman and, whatever her lifestyle, did not deserve to die like this. Thank you."

"Good one, boss. Let's hope for some results."

The phones were quiet. The crew were exchanging glances "is this a waste of time?", then one then another rang.

"Bournemouth Police. You're through to....."

Andy, Polly and I walked round the desks, eavesdropping on the conversations, hoping for a result. Some of the calls were nutters confessing. A few phoned through to tell us we had a voodoo cult operating in town. Then BINGO! Alison got excited and waved us over.

"Alison. Transfer to my office."

Andy, Polly followed me in and I waited for the call to be put through. As soon as it was, I switched to speaker. Polly sat with her notepad. Andy switched on the recorder.

"Hello. This is Detective Chief Inspector Morgan. May I know your name?"

"I'd rather not say."

Through my open door I could see Alison organising the trace.

"OK. That's fine. What is it you have to tell us?"

"I knew Mariana. It was a shock when I saw her photo on the news. Look, I'm a married man and it can't be known I visited Mariana on occasion."

"As I said, we know how to keep confidential. Please continue. We're grateful to you for calling in."

"OK. I like sex a certain way. Nothing weird. I just like the woman to be.. a bit tarty – fishnet stocking, loads of makeup, that sort of thing. My wife doesn't understand my need so I went on a website and looked up local prostitutes who did roleplay. I phoned a number – it was Mariana – made an appointment, and visited her about once a month. She was very good."

"Can you tell me Mariana's phone number? Only it will confirm we are talking about the same person... and the website."

The caller gave both details and it was indeed Mariana and now we had a website to check out.

"Look. I am going to ask a favour. And I promise we will be discreet. Would you meet me? Just me. Somewhere neutral."

"I'd rather not."

"Listen to me for a moment. If you phoned Mariana, we will have your number in the records. We will have to follow up all her callers and that may prove uncomfortable for some. If you meet me, I'd like to talk face to face. Give me your number. I won't share it with anyone and when we look at the phone contacts, I can take yours off. We'll not be calling at your home or place of work. This is the best for you."

There was a pause as the caller considered before he answered. "You promise?"

"One hundred percent. We're not interesting in harassing innocent people caught up in this. We only want to catch a brutal murderer."

"OK. Can you meet me now. I can let my wife know I'll be late home from work."

"That will do for me. Where?"

"ASDA car park at the station. Ring me when you arrive there." and he provided his mobile number.

"Thank you. I'm leaving now." and hung up.

"Polly and I will take our cars and stake it out. Give us five minutes head start."

"Yes. Go, go .go."

Alison called in from the outer office. "Got his number and checking name and address." The number matched the one he had given me.

"Good. Do that but keep it to yourself. He's not a suspect at the moment.."

CHAPTER 16

I pulled off the dual carriageway into the ASDA car park and did a drive through. I spotted a man near the trolley bank, looking uncomfortable and scanning vehicles. Stopping where he couldn't see me, I rang Polly.

"I'm here. Where are you?"

"Hi, boss. I'm eyes on the exit lane. "

"OK. I'm going to pick him up and once he's in the car we're going to the flat. Follow us. I'll have Andy on my open phone to listen to our conversation."

I hung up on Polly and phoned our witness.

"Hi. This is Inspector Morgan. I'll be coming in along by the trolleys. I'll flash once. Get in when I pull up. OK?"

"Yes."

I then phoned Andy. "He's waiting by the trollies. I'm going to pick him then once he's in the car I'll drive to Mariana's flat. Watch to see if anyone takes an interest in us then meet us there. Polly is going to tail me. I'm keeping my phone is on so listen in but don't speak. Got it?"

"Roger that."

I popped the phone in my shirt pocket with the microphone facing away from my body so as not to muffle it., before driving up to the trolleys, remembering to flash. The guy looked extremely nervous, as might be expected. Not a big man by any means. I leaned over and opened the passenger door. "Get in." which he did. "Do up your seatbelt."

"Why. Where are we going?"

"We can't sit here and chat. Too public and there is CCTV. Two men talking in a car might draw the wrong attention whereas a mate giving a mate a lift is innocuous."

That relaxed him a bit.

"Call me Harry." a further move to calm him down and draw him in. "Tell me how you contacted Mariana." I continued driving and, as yet, he didn't pay attention to our direction.

"I googled websites for sexual services. I found one that had it's own search engine for checking local services. I was able to click on a profile that looked interesting then send messages to say what I was after. Mariana agreed to meet me and gave me her phone number. The first time I went, I phoned for directions then again when I arrived in the street to say I'd arrived."

"No safety precautions on her part?"

"She gave me a code word to use when I knocked on her door. I guess she could see me from her window and check me out. I knocked on the door, gave the code word and she let me in. Hey, where are we going?"

"Relax, mate. We're going to the flat. I need you to look around, tell me if you see anything new or different. It's perfectly safe."

"I didn't agree to that."

"No backing out now. Just ten minutes, you and I. Honestly, you could help us break this case. "

I pulled up in the cul-de-sac. I had seen Polly behind me most of the way and she now overshot the cul-de-sac entrance so as not to follow me in. From the boot of my car I took masks, gloves and shoe slipovers.

Outside the door of Number 16 I put my set on and instructed my companion to do the same.

"OK. You knock on the door. Mariana asks for the codeword or do you just say it?

He thought. "I say it. She was waiting inside, knowing I was on my way up."

I opened the door with the keys I had brought out of Evidence. "Don't touch anything. Stick your hands in your pockets." It wasn't fingerprints I was concerned about – he had the gloves on – but sticky fingers maybe collecting a souvenir. We went inside the flat. "Give the history of that first visit, when you had never been before."

"We'd agreed on-line what I wanted, so she was already dressed a bit slutty. Little mini-skirt, fishnet stockings, bright red lipstick. She took me into the lounge and asked for the money."

"How much did she charge?"

"Sixty quid that time. Later she agreed on forty, when I promised to be a regular."

"You haggled on the price?"

"Not haggled. No. I explained I had limits on how much cash I could afford. I would draw cash every payday for the month, to buy lunches et cetera and I could hide forty pounds by skipping snacks and drinks."

"Right. Go on."

"She put the money under the clock on the mantelpiece and asked me if I wanted a drink."

"Did you?"

"Yes. She had a choice of spirits in that cupboard. I had a whisky."

We'd examined the cupboard and fingerprinted the bottles.

"Did you touch the bottles or did Mariana pour?"

"Mariana. After the drink we went into the bedroom."

"Let's go there. You lead."

He went unhesitatingly out of the lounge to the bedroom but paused before the door. I reached past him and opened the door, letting him stand in the door way examining the room. The bed was bare, all the linen had been taken for forensic examination along with the headboard.

He noticed it was missing and said so.

"Anything else?"

He took his time looking at the room. I was unsure he was trying to recollect or have a trip down memory lane, or sheer fascination he was at the scene of a horrible crime. Eventually, he spoke.

"I can't see anything different. But I wasn't really paying attention to the room."

"You'd have sex on the bed?"

"Yes. Mariana insisted on a condom. It went in that bin when we finished."

"Did you go in any other room when you were here? Kitchen? Bathroom?"

"Bathroom. Clean off after. Sometimes I would take a shower so I didn't smell of her perfume when I got home. I asked who else lived here."

"Why was that?"

"I could see a razor and men's toiletries in the bathroom. She said not to worry. A male friend sometime stayed but he knew to keep away when she was entertaining."

That didn't add much to our knowledge. By now we'd matched the shaving kit to Fox, whom we knew was sharing the flat.

83

"Anything else you can add? You've been really helpful."

"No. No, that's it. Are we done?"

"We're done. Thank you." I opened the front door. Andy and Polly were standing there and Mariana's punter shrunk back, scared.

"It's alright, mate. Andy here is going to take you back to your car. If you remember anything, Andy will give you a direct contact number."

"You won't be contacting me at home or work will you?"

"I don't expect to but if I have to, I'll phone you and you can say it's a wrong number and phone me back. We're grateful for your bravery in stepping up. Appreciate it can't have been easy. Andy. Run him back to ASDA. His car is in the carpark." I gave Andy a half wink. "OK, my friend, hand your mask and gloves to Andy. He'll dispose of them safely." meaning Forensics would collect his DNA for analysis and comparison.

Polly and I stood outside the door, while I hung up my open phone to Andy.

"What are you thinking, boss."

"I don't think the guy acted altruistically. Either he knew he could show up on our radar and wanted to forestall us arriving at his home or he wanted a bit of a thrill."

"Person of interest?"

I pulled a face. "Doubtful. He's not got the build to be the killer. That's no to say, deliberately or accidentally, he assisted the killer...... Poll. Time for some roleplay. You be Mariana. I'll be the killer. Go inside."

Polly looked at me, in gloves and overshoes and raised an eyebrow.

"No. It's alright. The place has been forensiced out. This was window dressing for the punter. I want him to think we might still find DNA or fingerprints, and Andy, right now is bagging the gloves and mask to go to Forensics."

Polly smiled and went inside, closing the door. I counted to five then knocked.

"Mariana. It's me."

Polly opened the door. "Well, hello handsome."

"Don't ad lib too much. Think how Mariana might have spoken."

"Sorry." she shook herself as if physically taking in the role."Well, hello. Come in."

I entered and Polly shut the door. I stood in the hallway.

"She would have taken the punter into the lounge to conduct the financial arrangement."

Polly went past me and into the lounge, I followed. She stood in the middle with her hand held out.

"Fifty pounds."

"Reasonable." I mimed taking out a wallet and counting out notes. "Put it under the clock."

Polly playacted.

"There was no money there, Poll, so our killer must have picked up."

"You're assuming he paid. We have no evidence of that."

"You're right. I was assuming he presented as a punter. We need parallel thinking. If he was a paying customer, it would be fantastic to find him with the notes in his wallet with Mariana's DNA on them."

"Too much time gone. He may have spent. He may have banked them. They've gone into the economy."

"Be nice though." I mused, before continuing. "Mariana might have offered a drink out of that cupboard. That could be how he got the rohypnol into her."

Polly had a different idea. "That would rely on him knowing she would have drink available. Our guy is a planner. I bet he brought a drink with him, already spiked. He would pretend to drink while she knocked hers back. Washed up the glasses, took the bottle away."

"Yeah, Sounds correct. So Mariana has taken the drug, falls unconscious or at least no resistance. A fall could explain the head injury. Have the records checked to see if any hair or blood found on the furniture, particularly the fireplace."

"I'd remember that. No, everything was clean. But I will check to where bleach was used."

"Good. So now he has Mariana unconscious. Undresses her."

"Not easy on a limp body."

"Guy said she was already in costume for him. If prearranged she might already be naked or just dressed in a robe."

"He chokes her. On the floor or on the bed?"

"Floor I think. He'd want to dress the bed in the black sheet before he placed her. He'd have been carrying a biggish bag. Shopping bag or gymbag. Dead cockerel, brand new sheet, still wrapped, and a knife minimum. If we get a bag it might be very revealing."

"So now he has a dead body. He makes up the bed. Mariana was into fetish. Why did he bring some props and not use what was here? I"ll ask Harding whether black candles appear in any of the porn movies. We assume Mariana's but the killer may have supplied those."

86

"He lifts her on the bed. Crosses her legs, puts her arms out. Puts the cord around her neck tightly. To ensure she has died or dressing? "

"I think he's confident she is dead. Goes into the kitchen to wash the glasses and put them away. Maybe tidy the lounge if anything disturbed, collect his money."

" When does he knife her?"

"The very last thing. If anyone should turn up, Mariana would look like she was sleeping. Plus, when the knife goes in, the heart has long stopped pumping so no spray. This man is dangerous. Calm. A planner. Is it a kink? I'd be amazed if this is his first murder. He's too calm. No hesitation."

"Perhaps we should ask Interpol? He might be clean in the UK but committed crimes abroad. This murder is something different. It almost as if he is challenging us, or laughing at us."

"I think you're right, Poll. We must spread the net. Something to do in the morning. In the meantime, I haven't eaten. Care to join me for an Indian, there's a good restaurant nearby? My treat."

"Sounds good, but on two conditions."

"Name them."

"I pay my way. I don't want gossip at work."

"Deal... except I pay for drinks. And the other?"

"No shop talk."

"Agreed."

Luckily we didn't need a reservation. The Taj was half full and the greeter, assuming we were a couple put us some distance from the other diners. Classic Indian restaurant décor – reds and pictures of the Taj Mahal taken at various times of day and seasons.

"I've not been here before," said Poll.

"Nor me. Ray Axel recommended it. He knows all the best places. What you having to drink?"

"Lager, I suppose. I'm having a curry."

"Me too. Two lagers, please. We'll call you back when we've chosen." The only time I would drink lager. A waiter came to the table with poppadums and a dish of chutneys.

There was a heck of a list on the menu cards but I chose a vegetable Balti and Polly had a Rogan Josh, naan breads for both of us. We did more eating than talking. It was actually quite relaxing and felt normal.

CHAPTER 17

I wonder if Harry would ever make a play for me. I sense a need in him and also a sadness. What would I do if he did? He's good-looking in a non-movie star way– real man – and I don't think Jason Statham is going to turn up.

I hadn't had much success finding a real man, a gentleman. Max was fine until he drank then the demons came out. I'd seen Harry angry but he channelled that to get results. I'd also seen him wipe away tears at some of the scenes we came across in the job.

Maybe it's normal to fancy your boss a little if he has the qualities you seek in a partner. I'd worked in other squads before but none had ever felt like this one – we really operated as a team, could finish each other's sentences, did things before we were asked. Andy was a great organiser, very patient and methodical. And you'd want him at your side if things kicked off. The new boy, Phil, was a tech wonder. The things he could do with a computer and the internet. I think he hero-worshipped Harry.

As for Harry, losing Lorraine was a terrible blow. It changed him. It was rare for him to relax off the job and the meal last night had been one of those occasions when he wasn't a policeman but just a man dining out with a woman.

Not a date.....not a date.......

CHAPTER 18

Pleasant as it had been to have a meal out with Polly as company and to talk about everyday things, once back in my flat I was unable to sleep and needed to run things through my mind. At my request, Alexa provided Satie's Gymnopedies and I poured a generous glass of 15 year old Glenfiddich to which I added two icecubes. Collecting an A4 writing pad and pen, I sat in the most comfortable chair and pondered, first savouring the bouquet of the single malt and anticipating the right moment to start drinking, when the ice has cooled the liquor and diluted it enough for smoothness, while I waited for inspiration.

The investigation was stymied by the uniqueness (as far as we knew at that moment) and the care of the murderer to avoid leaving a physical trace. There would be one – Edmond Locard's rule of every contact leaves a trace; the criminal leaves something at the scene and takes something from the scene away – but we didn't know what that trace was, so we preserved and catalogued everything. Carpet fibres were taken in case, when we had a suspect, we could find them on him or her. DNA samples from surfaces likely to have been touched by the killer. With only the one murder to investigate, we had no pattern. We needed to identify the relationship between killer and victim, how they made contact, where and when. I looked ahead, optimistically, to a day when we were in court and every strand of evidence sewed the case up against the defendant. Even with a confession, hard, physical evidence is desirable. Juries like that.

They also like motive, which we didn't have either. That might be the last thing we discover. The forensic trail was the way to go. I noted an Action Plan for the morning.

My glass was empty and I was wide awake, even at 1.00 a.m. so I logged in on my computer and, on a hope, googled crucifixion pictures, just in case the killer had a fixation and maybe planning more murders based on deaths of saints – a sign how desperate I felt.

The search results were overwhelming, chiefly in thanks to the Catholic faith. I had no faith. As a kid I'd ticked C of E on documents et cetera and sang the hymns in school assembly but we never went to church as a family and when I finally got more time with my father, him having retired from the Navy, he said he couldn't believe in a God who let the bad things he's seen happen. Mum was more of a Buddhist, at least in the philosophies. When she passed, we had a Humanist funeral and it felt more personal to us and not a script that a priest used endlessly at every oration.

I finally fell asleep. I dreamed of a shadowy figure, always out of grasp, elusive like smoke. A drum beat, like a pulse.

At work the next morning, it turned into a "Tech Day".

Instructed the collection of all mobile phone numbers of neighbours in the cul-de-sac so we could ignore them when mapping., although some would refuse to volunteer their numbers. Harding said "No problem. Eighty or more percent usage will be close to home, so I can look for saturation in that postcode and add to the database." I wish I understood him.

Harding had been awarded help to set up a database of all the phone numbers we came across so we could activate cross-referencing against multi-locations and Mariana's data. DC Dave Wilkins had been added to the team and we were glad to have him.

Harding was to look out for any phones on Pay-As-You-Go for likely burners (although in this neighbourhood, many would be PAYG, in order to avoid surprise bills). The kid was in his element so I left him to it.

Alex Dawson came up with more information. "We found a couple of hairs in the bedroom. Despite her lifestyle, Mariana was particularly clean. She may have had OCD if you consider how things were laid out in the rooms. She regularly cleaned her rooms. She may have been a junkie but she was aware of hygiene. Anyway, the hairs indicate African. There are three hair types, linked to ethnic origins and each has its own characteristics – particularly colour and texture. We can tell our samples are African as their unique characteristic is curly and kinky and with a flattened shape. The samples do not match Mariana, who is Caucasian, which is the most dense of the three types and is oval in shape. The three types cannot be confused."

"How does this help us. Alex? They could have been deposited anytime and missed in cleaning. Or fallen off clothing – secondary distribution."

"Oh, dear. Why didn't I think of that?"

"OK. What haven't you told me?"

I heard a chuckle at the end of the line before Alex answered. "The room was very clean. We did see vacuum marks on the carpet, you know, the tracks the brushes leave in the pile. So we took the vacuum cleaner into the lab, took it apart and checked the dirt collection. Nothing like these hairs found. So they were recent. OK, maybe not the killer but did he track in on his or her clothing? So either of black ethnicity or been in contact with. Ally that to the voodoo replication, it's worth investigating."

"It is, Alex. Thank you."

"One more thing. I've spoken to a uni friend of mine. He's a clinical psychologist. He's willing to have a word with you."

"We don't have the budget for that."

"No, it's alright. He'll take a phone chat as a favour. If things change and he can help, you can see about a budget later. Nothing to lose, Harry."

"OK. Give me his number and I'll call. He's expecting a call from me, is he?"

"I told him maybe."

"Cheers, mate. Owe you a drink."

I felt I owed it to Alex to at least check out his friend and a web search revealed that Brian Morrison was a Chartered Psychologist, a Fellow of the British Psychological Society and works in secure hospitals, prisons and courts and is a consultant for several police forces, had several papers published in the scientific community as well as being a rugby player in his youth (I thought I recognised the name).

I phoned Alex Dawson back.

"Alex. I'm going to pass on calling your friend. I think, based on the limited evidence we have it would be speculative. And there's the possibility a defence barrister could use it to put doubt in the jury's mind – 'You contacted a criminal psychologist but didn't present any evidence from him. Why was that? Did it not fit in with your theories?' - sort of thing.

"OK, Harry. Quite understand. How about I just have a colleague chat, no specifics and we talk about many issues not related to this case?"

"Tread carefully, Alex. Let me know, off the record, how it goes."

"Will do. Bye."

I continued with my research on the internet. It was fascinating to discover how little I knew about voodoo and how all of it came from movies, which generally focus on black magic. I started then to think our killer was using the scene setting, not as a real adherent but someone using the myth as their personal signature. The National Geographic website was particularly illuminating. Animal sacrifice is performed sometimes but the ceremonies do include Roman Catholic elements. Thinking about it, I did recall the Old Testament – Leviticus, I think - has clear instructions on animal sacrifice, so the similarities are not that far apart.

It was a while before I noticed Phil Harding was standing in my doorway.

"Yes, Phil? What is it?"

"I might have something, boss."

"ANDY! POLL! Get in here. OK, Phil, let's hear it."

"Well, I've been putting all the mobile numbers coming up into the database. I separate those known to belong to locals in the area pinged by the masts. That leaves me with visitors, fewer pings at each mast. I get down to one phone, one occasion at a mast. I then cross check each mast at an incident and one number came up at Dorchester and near the murder scene, our only match at both sites. It shows up twice near the flat, one of which was the night Mariana Gosling was killed."

"Good stuff. Do we have an owner?"

"No, sir. It was bought a month ago from a supermarket in London, a Pay-As-You-Go. I've asked how it was paid for and if the store has any CCTV from that date and time. I'm waiting to hear. If it is our guy, he'd have paid cash. He wouldn't slip up there. But we may get lucky with video."

Andy spoke. "Making some progress at last."

Harding continued. "There's more. I've been following the journey of the phone and collecting more data from the service provider. It started in London, goes around a bit, then drives down to Charminster, where it stays close by for a few days. Another track and trace shows the phone en route to Dorchester, near to the farm but not exactly – fewer masts in the countryside – and returning to Charminster. The right day for the rooster snatch. The next significant result is a visit to the vicinity of the flat the day before then again on the day of the murder. I can't place him in the Close, again it's the nearest mast. At the time of the murder, the same time Mariana's phone goes off service so does this one, within five minutes of each other."

"He's switched it off. Destroyed with Mariana's phone." Polly was probably right.

Andy interjected. "It's all very circumstantial, boss. We have to build up hard evidence around it."

Harding wasn't finished. "Charminster is the most stable site in the few days the phone was used. I have put masts on to a street map and drawn connecting lines and looked at the road layouts. It doesn't give me an address but looking at times et cetera, it does indicate he stayed with someone there in a very small neighbourhood span. If we can overlay any other intel on this, we may get a strong lead. "

"Our golden nugget would be to get one or both phones. That's a long shot but he may just keep them off-line 'til things cool down then start to reuse, or even sell on. Let's not give up hope. I feel we're getting lots of threads. Let's see if we can weave ourselves a noose from them, strong enough to convince a jury once we catch him."

"There's more, boss."

"What is it, Phil?"

"We used Martin Fox's phone as a gateway to Mariana's. I put his number in the database."

Andy, Polly and I had a strong air of expectancy, stimulated by the excitement coming off Harding, who continued. "I have our burner and Fox's phone off the same mast in Charminster. Charminster is not Fox's haunt , he sticks to Boscombe and the marinas for his boat, it doesn't fit in with other mast data."

There was silence in the room. We looked at each other. Finally, I found my voice.

"A connection or a coincidence?"

"Connection," said Andy.

"Connection," said Polly.

"Connection," I affirmed. "Phil. Get me a triangle of Gosling, Fox and Voodoo Man. I want to see how many points of similarities and how they intersect with each other. Good work. Bloody good work. Which database did you use?"

"My own, sir. I wrote one out for just such an occasion. The official ones don't have enough fields."

"Fields?"

"Think boxes. Each box contains a single point of information. Some databases squeeze too much into one box. I had individual fields for the phone numbers, brand of phone, type of phone, names if known, service provider, date of purchase, postcode by district and postcode by street.. I added mast locations by postcode. Then I instructed the database to organise, checking each field for matches."

"You lost me after 'boxes' but it seems to have worked. I'm afraid I need you write a report on this, in detail and layman's terms for when we present to the prosecutor and maybe to a jury."

"I'll get on it right away."

"Good man."

"But one more thing. If I could actually have Fox's phone and did he have a satnav in his car? I could really pin things down with those."

"Polly. Could you look into that? Great. OK. People, back to work."

As Polly exited, Sharon MacKay, my boss, came in, walked along the boards with casual examination then came over to my office.

"How's it going, Harry?"

"Sharon. Nice of you to pop down to the engine room."

"Not hearing much about progress, Harry. Thought I'd better drop by and see who needs a bit of motivation. You're using a lot of resources and resources cost. I can't have an open chequebook – we'll need money for other cases. The policing budget for Dorset has been cut yet again. We're looking at fighting crime with just fresh air."

Fair point. Dorset was one of the worst funded police forces. One large conurbation of the conjoined Bournemouth, Christchurch and Poole. Smaller towns like Dorchester, Weymouth, Shaftesbury and hundreds of square miles of rural communities. The latter had been suffering rustling on an industrial scale and soaking up resources without results. The farming lobby had a powerful voice and the Commissioner and Chief Constable were often vocally attacked for failure to put an end to it. I decided the sparring was over and brought MacKay up to speed.

"We are starting to make progress. The collection of evidence is like looking for, not a needle in a haystack, but a single piece of hay in a haystack. Just now, we may have made a breakthrough, but we have to follow it up. A person of interest has materialised – no name.
We have location data of this individual being in place for the stealing of the rooster at the farm and near the cul-de-sac. We may soon have data placing him with the victim's boyfriend, Martin Fox, who is presently awaiting trial for drug smuggling. Our approaches are to continue to place the suspect in locations that tie up and I will, when the time is ripe, approach Fox to spill the beans. I may have to talk to the Prosecutor to do a deal. Murder trumps drug smuggling. I hope I can count on your support ma'am."

MacKay had listened and I could almost see the cogs whirring in her head. A smuggler off the streets or a murderer caught – how did the scales tip with her superiors and with the public? Finally, she spoke, "Of course. Keep me informed." and she left.

After MacKay went, I sat and perused my team through the open door. I was assured with my choices. Andy Robins should make Inspector soon, he deserves the promotion, but I'd be sad to lose him. This is our biggest case. Crack this and he'll be headhunted. My loss, someone else's gain. Polly Polanski was a jewel. Not only a brilliant detective, she was hardworking and fearless and I appreciated her cheeky humour. Our biggest boon was the youngster, Phil Harding. His technical skills made things possible that the rest of us only dreamed of. I recalled some of his history. West Indian mother – Rose-Marie, whom I had met and charmed me. Father – Craig Harding, Dorset man and engineer and a maestro of the barbecue. Harding had exhibited an early interest in computers and was writing software at an early age. I believe he won a national award for something he'd done at school. Went to Technical College then University. More than a geek, he was a natural detective. I fancied that sometime in the future he might go private as a Consultant – his skills very much in demand as detective work can get so much from mobile phone data these days. I didn't ask (best not to know) but I suspected he kept contacts he made at uni and some of them would be hackers. The others had yet to show their potential but early signs were that Alison would rise through the ranks. She never turned down a task, often the first to volunteer and was a fan of Polly's, learning from her how to survive a male-dominated environment. Others were loans – helping to sort mountains of data – and would go back their posts after. I had an eye on Dave Wilkins who had diligently and intelligently worked on the Laura Jenkins missing child case. He might be a plodder but we need people to work slowly and not make massive leaps of deduction.

Later, I received a phone call from Alex Dawson. "Harry. It's about time we met up for coffee."

I was about to say I was too busy then the penny dropped – Alex wanted to chat away from the office, informally. "OK. How about in the coffee lounge of the hotel? I'll call when I get there and you only have to pop over the road."

That agreed, I told Andy I was popping out but to call me if any breakthroughs. It took twenty minutes to get to the hotel from the office. I phoned Alex from the carpark then went in and ordered a large Americano for him and double espresso for me plus two Danish pastries. With any luck, Alex would not be hungry and I would eat both. He came in just as I was carrying our coffees to a quiet space away from other customers. Sadly, he tucked into a Danish immediately and wolfed it down. "Sorry, skipped lunch." I pushed the second one over to him.

"I trust this is not just to get me to treat you?"

"Not at all. I phoned my friend and we chatted about symbolism for killers in general terms – I didn't mention any specifics from our case. We got round to Christian symbols and rituals and I snuck in voodooism. Apparently, you should forget any horror films you've seen. Voodoo, or Vodou as it is better known by adherents, is a fusion of old faith taken by slaves to the plantations and mixed there with Christianity, usually Catholic. Modern Vodou ceremonies involve Catholic prayers. It's main tenet is everything is spirit. Humans are spirits who live in the visible world, and they worship the one true God. Forget devil worship. That myth came about when outsiders witnessed ceremonies and assumed the worshippers were making a pact with the devil. They do sacrifice animals. It's to provide sustenance to spirits not in physical form and usually provides a meal for the congregation after."

"In Leviticus, there are precise instructions for animal sacrifice and Judaism and Islam both have rules for ritual slaughter, so nothing really bizarre there. But our guy was window dressing – no signs of ceremony. "

"Agree. The other information confirms the expectation the killer is male. Statistics point by a huge margin to it not being a woman, add that to the strength needed to strangle, lift the body on the bed and penetrate through the chest with a knife is either male or a Russian female athlete."

"So let's run this through. We're looking, with a high probability, for a male of African ethnicity..."

"The hairs." Alex nodded.

"...who may have West Indian connections for knowledge, however imperfect of Voodoo..."

"Or a film collection of George Romero or Hammer"

".....and is sending a message to someone. "

"He might think he knows voodoo – a little knowledge, enough to impress people he wants to control. Maybe claim supernatural powers, being a spirit who walks the earth."

"He seems like a spirit. A real shortage of tangible evidence. We aren't even certain the hairs are his until we can cross reference with other evidence."

"Can't help you there, Harry, until you find me more stuff."

"I wonder what the mix is with ethnic criminals. Do whites mix with blacks n the same gang? My experience is types stay firm. Alliances might be 'ormed but the hard core are always 'family'."

I looked, with some regret, at the last surviving crumbs of the pastries and bid farewell to Alex to head back to the office.

CHAPTER 19

Joseph screamed again as the leather strap wielded by his grandmother came down across his back. It was a strap made for the purpose, not a repurposed belt and his mother, as a child, had known its bite.

"You're a wicked boy. Repent," Nana screamed as she landed another blow across his buttocks.

The eight year old writhed in pain, as much as he had freedom to do so, being held down by his grandfather.

"I didn't do anything, nana."

"Liar. You will go to hell," and she started reciting prayers, each sentence another blow. Only when she was exhausted would she stop. This was a regular occurrence in the household, his back was already scarred from beatings.

Joseph's mother Mayleen, at sixteen, had snuck out of the house to go to a party. Excited to be among older teenagers and young men and women, booze and marijuana had caused her downfall and a night of sex was the result. She'd been flattered by the attention paid her by the host, the oldest male there at thirty. He'd held court and handed out cocaine liberally. At first, she thought it was just going to be heavy-petting, but he had taken her into a bedroom and stripped her, let her lick the white powder off his chest, handed her glasses of vodka. Her first real sexual experience was fuelled by the heavy combination and the thought she was being treated as an adult, an equal. A small pang of fear when his heavy rection was held in front of her face, before he flipped her over and took er from behind. A brief start of pain as she lost her virginity, quickly naesthetised by the stimulants. She clawed the sheets as he rode her, eaching his climax with a roar, withdrawing then slapping her buttocks as e did.

"Go, girl. Yo the best."

But she had passed out.

When her monthly visitor didn't appear she confided in a friend.

"Honey. We need to get you a test."

Mayleen was pregnant. She went to the flat where the party had been eld. The man who had treated her to the drugs and drinks was laid on a ofa, dressed only in shorts and empty beer cans around his feet. Jamal /as a later riser, having spent the night and evening partying and dealing.

"You is over sixteen, ain't ya, girl?"

"Last November. What you going to do?"

"Ain't my problem. Probably ain't my kid."

Mayleen felt suicidal but her friend took her in. Eight months later she ave birth to Joseph.

His father became slightly interested because of state benefits. Living /ith him, Mayleen became an addict and, when Joseph was hardly a year ld, fatally overdosed.

Grandma found her grandson tied to her front door handle. She saw im as the result of the sin of her only daughter.

Nana was a strong disciplinarian and, for all the obedience to the Bible ("spare the rod, spoil the child" she saw as an warning and not an instruction) she had strong beliefs in witchcraft and it was her mission to chase the devil out of the children with a heavy leather strap. As well as asking the priest to bless them and their compulsory Sunday attendance at church, she held private rituals in the house. Neighbours would come to have their fortunes told or for spells. It was a lucrative business.

Joseph would witness other beatings – local families with a "problem" child came to have the demons beaten out of them. On those occasions, Joseph was made to perform the services of an "altar boy" - lighting candles then holding down the child while his grandmother laid on with the strap. To the families, it had the appearance of effectiveness – few children wanted to be taken to visit the Mambo – the priestess – for a second whipping. Grandma had a cupboard full of accoutrements, locked. On the walls of the house were crucifixes and icons, and the local Catholic priest would be a frequent visitor, ignoring the situation, because his congregation was large and he would hide his doubts in the bottle.

By his twelfth birthday, Joseph had outgrown his peers and with a propensity for sports, was physically fitter than most.. Grandma promoted him from "altar" boy to associate priest and he learned the rituals, sometimes taking turns with the strap as age began to tell on the old lady, who was having irregular heart rhythms. He could not be washed of the sin of being a bastard but he was useful to keep the money coming in. Joseph could see the fear on the faces of children brought in for treatment but he could afford no mercy, and in time he became immune to any such feelings. He did what he had to to survive.

Grandfather, who was a lot older than Nana, worked on the railways, along the lines. One day there was an incident where he fell under a train and died from his injuries. Nana was awarded generous compensation and bought their house. That raised the respect in the community and some suspected she had cast a spell to make it happen. Her power was never stronger.

She trained Joseph in the deeper rituals and, with his imagination, he built up an aura around himself at the ceremonies. He subtly let it be thought that Nana was the earthly presence of Maman Brigitte, a divine being of the Underworld and the mistress of Baron Samedi. Her animal associate was a black rooster and one day Joseph acquired one. Joseph was suspected of being taken over during ceremonies by a loa, a divine being that acted as intermediary between man and gods.

Shortly after his fourteenth birthday, Joseph saw his Grandma collapse and die, her heart gave out. Before the body was taken to the church for the funeral service, Joseph held a Vodou service in the house. It was well attended, a long line of people filing through the house and the mourners filled a pot with cash to ask for her intervention in their problems from "the other side".

Social Services would have stepped in at this time, but Jamal, his biological father, turned up, having heard the news of the death and *claimed parental rights. Not out of love but the opportunity to have a house and claim benefits. The side line was drugs. Joseph's father was a small player in the local scene and local boys he used as runners were in and out of the house all the time.*

Joseph kept up the Vodou as an earner. His father had him hold ceremonies over his gang members, convince them of his power and the danger if they ever crossed him.

CHAPTER 20

When I got back in the office it was to be told of some progress by Harding and his mini-team.

"Boss. I've got the shop's records of phones purchased with cash," Harding was keen to tell me. "Bad news is, it's the norm for the neighbourhood. Locals are in the low economy bracket, cash in hand jobs, can't get credit cards et cetera." Cheeky bugger kept me hanging for a bit before he hit me with the best bit. "The shop has CCTV, inside and out. Shoplifting and vandalism. Want to see what I've got?"

I couldn't get to his desk side quick enough, where Andy and Polly joined us. Harding clicked his mouse and his PC screen opened up and a video ran. We watched a large black male, baseball cap low and head down, no logos on his clothes, plain windcheater and jeans. The shopkeeper made the sale and the next clip was the street outside, where the buyer of the phone walked down the road and got into an Audi saloon, number plate not readable at the distance as the focus was set for the immediate store front and pavement. CCTV footage was monochrome, so we didn't even have a colour for the car.

I rubbed my chin in thought. Everyone was quiet. Finally, I spoke.

"Right. This ticks a few boxes but is not conclusive. Phil. Set up searches on routes from London into Dorset for Audis – saloons, not SUVs or estates. Is that too much?"

"No, boss. A lot of work but doable. I'll start with the M27 from Southampton to Dorset as the lesser traffic matching the times we have for the phone journey then look for the vehicles from London that match."

"Good. Andy. Ask Traffic if any number plate recognition vehicles or cameras about in the period of interest. See if they have any records of Audis with London addresses."

"On it."

Harding was not done. "I'll search all masts en route from London to Dorset to follow the phone number. If I get anything, it will give me the times of the journey and shorten the CCTV searches."

"Brilliant. Let's do it."

I felt we were on the verge of a potential breakthrough. From almost zero to proper leads to follow felt good. Andy asked for a quiet word.

"Boss, I can't do evening. Maureen got us tickets for a concert. I can't go with her because the babysitter fell through and Mo's expecting me to stay home with the kids. I don't want to let her down – she's been looking forward to this for months. Is that OK?" He looked worried that I'd insist he did the evening stint.

"No, Andy. You and Mo go to the concert. I'll come round and sit the kids. They'll be in bed and no trouble. I can bring my laptop and work from there."

"Harry, you're a marvel. I'll phone Mo now. Thanks, boss."

Polly, who had overheard us, gave me a big grin.

True to my word, I turned up in time. The twins had had a bath and were all wrapped up in their pyjamas and dressing gowns. Maureen gave me a big kiss on the cheek and her and Andy were off in a taxi. I forgot to ask hat the concert was. Ritual was to tuck the twins in bed, read them The ruffalo (doing different voices, which made them giggle), then turn the nain light off, leaving a night light that shone Disney characters on the wall nd ceiling.

"Now, sleep tight, ladies. I'll be downstairs if you need me."

"Goodnight, uncle Harry, " simultaneously.

I closed the door, leaving a gap so I could hear them if necessary.

In the lounge I set up my laptop and started going through the files. I ked to set up a progress report for myself, it helped to keep my mind from vandering across details. An hour had passed when there was a tap on ne window. Cautiously, I drew back a curtain and, in the light spilling out, I aw it was Polly. With a big grin she held up a pizza box. I went and let her n.

"Andy phoned me from the taxi. Said they forget to leave you any supper ecause all this was last minute."

Delicious smells were coming from the box, so we both went into the itchen. While Polly organised plates, I found a bottle of red in Andy's wine ack and pulled the cork. Carrying food and drink, Polly and I went back to ne lounge. I paused at the bottom of the stairs – all quiet.

Polly looked at the laptop. "No Netflix?" I shook my head. "Must be porn nen."

"Not tonight, Poll. My subscription has run out."

The banter over, we devoured the pizza and half the bottle.

"Pick a DVD, Poll. My head is spinning from all these files. Need to witch off."

Polly picked Ghost. I hadn't seen that for years - last time was with my vife. We sat on the sofa, volume low so we could hear if the girls woke.

109

The time passed quickly. I hadn't had normality like this for some time. The film ended too soon.

"I'd better go, Harry. Busy tomorrow."

"Stay for coffee?"

"Better not. Need my beauty sleep. See you in the morning."

She let herself out and I heard her start her car and drive away. I suddenly felt very lonely. I looked at the remaining half bottle but resisted, knowing I'd be driving home. I must have dozed on the sofa, because the next thing, Maureen was gently shaking me awake.

"Harry, Harry."

"Maureen. You're back. What time is it?"

"One a m. Do you want me to make up the spare bed?"

"No, I'll be fine. I'll get off home. Was it good?"

"Brilliant. We owe you, Harry."

"No. Family, Mo. Family." I kissed her on the cheek, picked up my laptop and met Andy in the hallway, coming in from paying the taxi.

"Everything OK? Kids no problem?"

"Fine. Polly rescued me with a pizza and stayed a while."

"I owe her. We hadn't organised supper, not having a babysitter. I only realised in the taxi."

"No problem, Andy." and it wasn't. The team looked out for each other. Family.

The next morning we assembled in my office. Harding looked like he'd pulled an all-nighter.

"I searched the main route down from London, M3, M27, A31. I tracked the phone and gave the times to Traffic to look through their records. We picked up several Audis but only one saloon at the London end and here in town.....We got a plate."

We didn't actually high five each other, but spiritually we did.

"Well done, Phil. Bloody marvellous. Let the others go back over the local cameras around the flat. You go home and get some rest. You look done in." I patted him on the shoulder.

"Thanks, boss. Appreciated."

Looking half dead, he took himself off. I'd be putting a recommendation in.

Andy said it. "Where would we be without the technology? Old school methods wouldn't stand a chance today."

"We're the Sweeney! You're nicked!" Andy and Polly looked at me without comprehension. "I used to watch it with my father. It's repeated on one of the channels showing old programmes."

"Whatever."

"Coffee, everyone?"

CHAPTER 21

I was lucky to have ended up on Harry Morgan's team. I was learning a lot from him. I would never want to disappoint him. The time I'd spent in uniform was okay, I only ever met a little discrimination for being mixed-race, usually some old guy having had too many lagers would comment but my colleagues had my back.

My skills with the technology got me quickly into CID and the boss had asked for me to be on his team. It's a good team. Andy and Polly are devoted to him and he has the loyalty of all who work for him. Alison worships him from afar, almost a crush. I'd like to ask her out on a date but worry about rejection and spoiling the atmosphere in the office.

Mum and Dad had wanted to meet my colleagues and I suggested a barbecue, which replaced the end-of-case session in a boozer. Dad was a master of the outdoor grill and kept everyone fed. Harry had turned up with cases of beer, which we put in a tin bath and covered with ice from the supermarket. I think Mum fell a little bit in love with the boss. Afterwards, Dad said I had fallen in with a good crowd and he was pleased I was enjoying my career.

I'd never want to disappoint the boss or let my colleagues down.

CHAPTER 22

Phil Harding turned up early the next morning, looking totally revived. He said he'd crashed as soon as he got through his front door and slept for twelve hours solid, got up and worked on his database remotely, went back to bed and slept to 4 in the morning. Up and went out for a run, came home showered and was at his desk at 7.

A courier turned up at 9 with Martin Fox's phone; I'd asked for a favour and got one. I took it over to Harding.

"We've got this for a couple of hours before I have to get it back. It's Fox's. What can you do with it."

Harding was already connecting to his PC as he replied. "It's Android and Google will have tracked the places he visited. I can check the GPS, photos files, and calls made if he hasn't wiped. What's the passcode?" He saw my face and got his answer."No worries, boss."

I watched him try the obvious stuff – 0000, 1111, 2222 through to 9999 – without success.

Next effort was Fox's birth year, and variations of same, even reversing.

"Dead end, then?"

"Not necessarily." Our own tech wizard then rang the phone using some software on his PC (which I had never seen on mine, but best not to ask questions.)

Fox's phone rang and Harding answered it. "Now I have an open line I can get inside it and find what we want."

I thought it best not to be around. "Off the record, Phil. Handwrite down what you find and give to me and only me."

"Boss."

I went back in my office to wait and pretend to be busy, because I really had nothing to do until we had more to go on. Polly brought me a coffee and a KitKat chocolate biscuit.

"Thanks, Poll. Got time to listen to a theory?"

"Only if you share the KitKat. It's the last one."

Luckily it was a four finger bar.

"I started to watch King Lear on Prime last night, the version with Anthony Hopkins. It reminded me of when Lorraine and I went to Chichester to see Frank Langella play the role. A tour-de-force. Anyway, scene one and I started thinking, bloody hell how Trumpian is this?"

"Explain."

"We first meet Lear as a megalomaniac who desires and needs flattery. Then he splits up his territory between his children and their partners, but kicking one out. At the same time though, he wants all the trappings of a king just not the work."

"Interesting, but relevance?"

"Coming to it. But let me tell you about scene two first. We meet Edmond, a bastard son, who incidentally has a brilliant speech, as good as Shylock's 'if you prick us, do we not bleed?' " I could see I was losing Polly at this point. "Sorry. I am saying we need to understand all the characters in our crime. Not totally evil but dealing with the world their way... and I was going to mention that Edmond misled his biological father with some fake news."

At that moment, Andy Robins stuck his head round the door and Polly called out to him, "We have a new person of interest – King Lear."

Andy looked surprised, no wonder, so I hastened to continue. "Let's put the play aside. I was only illustrating how it sparked an idea. What if we have a crime lord protecting his interests but having tried to share out the work and it backfired? Mariana's death is an object lesson to somebody."

Andy perked up. "Like when Al Capone smacked that person over the head with a baseball bat in front of everyone." He looked slightly apologetic at our responses. " I saw The Untouchables."

Polly was getting behind the idea now. "Fake news. As in misdirection."

"Yes. We can't trust what we see because we don't know the actors and their motives."

Andy perked up. "We should be looking at big players, and that is most probably drug lords. "

"Speak to Ray Axel. See if he has anything that might give us some leads."

Andy phoned Ray. I wanted to stay free while waiting for the results from Harding, but I could hear the conversation.

"Hi, Andy. What can I do for you?"

"We have a theory that our murder could be drug gang related. We have our actor moving around Charminster before he visits the victim. He's been tracked down from London. The victim's boyfriend is a known smuggler and dealer – he's waiting trial as we speak."

"You may be on to something. Operation Iron Glove has been clamping down on the County Lines successfully. Hampshire Police covered Southampton and we picketed Bournemouth and Poole. Nicked quite a few – sadly just lads, not the bosses – but it's closed down the business a lot. Talking of Charminster, we're doing a raid over there tonight. Got a tip about business being conducted in a hairdresser's and we know the owner, got a bit of a record. The business is a front for dealing and money laundering. It's been under surveillance for a month and does little real business. Sent one of our girls in, undercover, but they wouldn't do her hair, power cut they said. We've seen customers go in and out but too quickly for a haircut and not looking any better on the way out than on the way in."

While Ray was bringing Andy up to speed on the scene. Harding had handed me his notes. I joined the conversation.

"Ray. It's Harry. Can we join you tonight? We've got extra interest on th Charminster scene now. The victim's boyfriend has been over there just before he was nicked. He was off his usual territory. It seems all roads lead to Charminster."

CHAPTER 23

I sat in Ray Axel's car. I wouldn't be at the forefront of the raid and my guys were in cars behind us. Ray would let us in after his team had finished and I would be able to go to the station to listen to the interviews. Through his windscreen, unusually clean for Ray, I could see along the street and a Hairdressing Salon, unlit, but lights on in the flat above. Ray gave me the background.

"We had a CI give up this place as somewhere drugs were sold. Did some checks and the owner has a record for prostitution. Unlikely she had the means to set up the business so there must be a backer. We're going in soon, strip the place for evidence, see where it all leads."

I gave him out intel. "Our phone chasing has this area of interest. Haven't pinged it to an exact address but very much on the doorstep. We've our London based suspect here as well as a local, who's currently inside for smuggling. It's his girlfriend who was murdered. So many coincidences – and I don't think they are."

Ray continued. "If we have an OCG, the previous owner, who was a genuine hairdresser, could have been forced out or paid off. She's moved to Spain and we're following up for her story. Current listed owner is Marie Franks and she used to use the flat for business and still occupies it. Her game was fetish sex – bondage, whipping. Higher income than straight sex and it doesn't hurt that she's a bit meaty."

"Meaty?"

"You know, packs a bit of weight. Handy for a dominatrix I should think."

"Each to their own, Ray. We have a witness to the lifestyle of our victim. He liked slutty tarts."

"Isn't that it? Best wife is Nigella in the kitchen and a tart in the bedroom? So they say....Oops, action!"

I could see a male, acting unusually cautious, walk down the street and round the back of the premises.

"Punter or addict. Night time access is at the rear." Ray got on the radio. "White male entering the premises. If he leaves, take him. We go in five."

I phoned Andy, who was waiting further back in his car, with Polly. "About to kick off, Andy. Sit and watch. I'll confirm when it's time for us to go in."

"Roger that, boss."

The male did not come out before Ray gave the signal.

"GO, GO, GO!"

Two unmarked vans came down the road at speed, screeched to a halt and discharged coppers in uniform and detectives in raid strip. Two of them covered the front door in case of escape and the rest piled round the back. We could hear the door being smashed in and cries of "Police!" as a warning to occupants.

Ray got a call on his radio. "We're in, boss. Place is secure. But you must see this."

We got out of Ray's car and I turned to join my crew.

"No, Harry. In with me. I'd like your eyes and brain on this."

I waved to Andy to stay put and trotted after Ray. We went down a blind alley, past bins and followed the directions of a constable, who used a torch to show us the way. Up a steel staircase and through the door into the flat. Ray's DS had a huge grin on his face as he pointed into a room. We found Marie Franks in black PVC and the white male we had observed earlier tied naked over a bench and several lines of weals across his buttocks. Apparently, Marie had not given up on the trade. Ray took charge.

"Release him. Get him dressed and down the station for a statement." The guy was whimpering, but whether from the punishment or the embarrassment and discovery.

Ray turned to Marie. "Right, sweetheart. Let's see what else you have on the premises. Do you want to say anything?"

"Not without a lawyer. And I want my phone call."

Ray turned to his DS. "Read her her rights and take her down the station. Don't put them in the same car. "

"Boss."

Everyone was pulling on gloves now, before we started searching. No need for full gear.

Videos were rolling and digital stills taken of everything. As drawers were opened an array of designer goods were discovered, far more than could be expected of a Salon Owner to afford, even a downmarket sex worker. One wardrobe revealed bundles of notes, enough to fill two kitbags. All was logged and put into evidence bags. We had a cry from the kitchen.

"Boss! In here."

Ray and I went through and laid out on the worktop, having been taken from a cupboard, were cellophane bags of white powder. Ray thumped the air. "Got it. Get it bagged and down to Forensics, I want a quick result of whether this matches any other finds. Let the fingerprint boys loose too."

Results were a lot quicker these days. We could expect answers within 48 hours. Instead of the messy dusting for prints, the first analysis would be to put items under light and go through the spectrum. The oils, sweat and dirt from fingers would hopefully show up and could be matched to ones on file. A further test, if the light trials were not successful were to put items in a chamber, play with the humidity and burn off superglue for the fumes, which would attach to the finger residue and could be photographed.

It was obvious that Marie was not as fussy about hygiene and cleanliness as Mariana. I had an idea - a longshot.

"Ray. Have the whips, canes and shackles bagged. It might prove useful to see if any skin cells on them with useful DNA. Just bagged for now, no need for the expense of the labs."

"Got it, Harry. Meet me at the station tomorrow. I want you in on the interviews".

"Wouldn't miss them. I'll be there bright and early."

CHAPTER 24

Once everyone was seated – Martin Fox and his solicitor, Ray Axel and myself – Ray switched on the machine and after a long beep to indicate it was working, Ray gave the date and time and names of all present, followed by the legal requirements and caution.

"Interview by Superintendent Axel and Detective Chief Inspector Morgan. Martin Fox, you do not have to say anything, but it may harm your defence if you do not mention when questioned something you later rely on in court. Anything you do say may be used in evidence. Welcome back, Martin. Your name came up in an investigation of dealing on premises in Charminster. You lead an interesting life."

Fox looked at Ray then me. His weaselly brain was working overtime. His lawyer spoke, a slick guy in a double-breasted suit, matching silk handkerchief and tie.

"Mr Fox is willing to answer your questions but would like to know what you offer in return."

Ray chuckled, which had the effect of rattling Fox, before answering.

"Your client must know what a mess he's got involved in. We already have him in possession and now we can tie him in with a major dealing operation and County Lines. We busted a hairdresser in Charminster, a front for major drug dealing, and the owner is singing like a canary. She put Martin's name in the frame big time. It's in his best interest to tell us everything and we can tell the judge he has assisted in our enquiries."

Ray pushed some photos over the desk — outside shots of the premises and what we had found inside.

The lawyer huddled in to Fox and whispered in his ear, getting a whisper back then turning to Ray and me. "Mr Fox is willing to answer your questions."

Ray was following PEACE — Plan, Explain, now Ask. We'd listen to Fox's account then Challenge it, before final Evaluation of the interview. I wouldn't be asking questions but I was keenly watching Fox's reaction (which was also being captured on camera) in order to spot misdirection c hiding something.

"Why don't you tell us your side of the story, Martin? What's your involvement?"

"Listen. I just did small stuff. Just bringing in a bit for locals, a few mates They recommended me to others and I had my trade. I met (pointing at the picture of the hairdresser) Marie through Mariana — they did skinflicks together once. She told me she had taken on the salon under her flat and was using it to distribute but needed a steady supply. The kids from London could only bring in small amounts and your lot were picking most up at the stations so she wanted a local."

"Go on."

"I was to bring the stuff in and she would distribute. I had a load and took it over. There was a big black there. Introduced himself as Joseph. Size of a truck. He'd bankrolled Marie and persuaded the original owner o the salon to sell up. He had an op in the City and was running County Lines until it became a target. His idea was to get me to collect and bring in on my boat. Laid it all out and I agreed."

"What more can you tell us about this Joseph character? Does he have a last name?"

"He never told me. Just called himself Joseph. Scary fucker." Fox rolled back the sleeve of his right arm. "He did this to me. " We could see a recently healed scar."Made me promise never to cheat him or rat on him at pain of death. He cut this on my arm, licked my blood then poured hot candle wax on it. It fucking hurt like hell."

"Go on, Martin. You're doing well."

"I'd made one delivery to the salon before you guys nicked me on my second run. That's all I did. "

"Martin. We want to know more about Joseph. We're not interested so much in you. The more you can tell us, the better it goes down for you."

"Can you protect me?"

"What?"

"Can you protect me? That fucker will carve me for dinner if I give him up. Don't you get it? Mariana was a warning for me to keep quiet."

Ray and I exchanged looks and I took over the questioning.

"Are you telling us Joseph killed Mariana?"

"Who else would have? I was inside and knew too much. He'd warned me that he was not to be crossed. When I heard how Mariana had died I just knew."

"Do you have any proof?"

"That's your job. I just know it. It was in his eyes that he could kill. For a big bastard he could move like a ghost. I wouldn't have ratted. He didn't need to kill Mariana. She was the only good thing in my life."

"Everything, Martin. Tell us everything you can. Accent? Jewellery. Tatts or markings."

123

"As I said, big fucker. You couldn't miss him. London accent. No tattoos or markings. He wore something weird on a gold necklace. A skull with a snake going in the mouth and out an eye socket. "

"Martin. We'll get an artist in. If you can describe the jewellery to him. And a photofit to help with his picture."

"OK. He drove an Audi. It was parked outside the salon when I arrived the first time."

CHAPTER 25

Joseph was a year older than Desmond, who saw the influence Joseph had over the neighbourhood. He knew he could learn from him, so he watched, asked questions, became Joseph's altar boy.

When the time came to move away and set up his own operation, Desmond changed his name to Joseph and took what he had learned of vodou and made it his signature. The original Joseph's reputation moved with the new Joseph.

Joseph mk2 took his experiences running for Jamal and started his own gang. Over time it grew and he used the vodou for control.

The market became the counties out of London. Coastal towns for the party people and especially if there were a university attached. Joseph started putting his boys on trains to go and deliver to a hungry clientele.

But the police started to arrest at numbers higher than his operation could withstand. He lost too many of his crew, too much merchandise confiscated. He needed a new arrangement – locals who could do the work.

His system was to get them to fear him but also respect him. He gave each a defence fund – a stash of money to hire the best solicitor if they were ever arrested for dealing.

Joseph eyed the small ratty guy. He'd be no threat but could he do the job?

Marie Franks was proposing him as their runner. Fox could ship the drugs around the County Lines cops, pick it up at one marina and bring into

Poole. He could even avoid docking at the main sites, Poole Bay being so
shallow except where dredged for the ferries and commercial vessels.
Lots of small charter fishing boats as well as the shellfish guys. He
seemed quite confident and his eyes had lit up at the size of business
Joseph was talking and the profits involved.

Looking at Franks then Fox, Joseph decided they were not a couple.
He'd want some leverage – family, kids – to hold over him. Taking out a
bottle of vodka and filling glasses , he produced some high grade
marijuana to smoke – a "sample". Fox partook eagerly and under the
influence talked. Joseph learned about a girlfriend – Mariana – and her
lifestyle, which was added to when Franks explained her connection and
how she knew Franks. Fox was even so boastful he showed Joseph
Mariana's advert on a porn site. Joseph memorised the details.

Marie went into the kitchen to add ice to the drinks. Joseph said to Fox
he must swear loyalty. Fox said, of course. Joseph took out a red candle
from his carry-bag and lit it. Fox looked apprehensive at this strange turn,
especially when Joseph started chanting in strange language. He did not
have the strength to resist when Joseph grabbed his arm and took out a
flick-knife and slashed a cut. The drug dulled his senses but when hot
candle wax was poured over the wound Fox cried out. Joseph smiled.

"Our deal is sealed. You work for me and cheat me at your peril. I own
your soul."

CHAPTER 26

The next interview was with the hairdresser- Marie Franks. Another solicitor – this time a woman, two piece suit and pearl necklace. Expensive perfume – not overwhelming but subtle floral tones that don't come cheap.

Ray read the charges and the caution before asking Franks if she wanted to make a statement.

"No comment."

"Marie. We have you bang to rights. It won't help you to stay silent."

The solicitor spoke: "My client is not obliged to say anything and reserves her right to remain silent at this time."

"That's OK then. I'll just walk you through the evidence and any time, Marie, you feel like chipping in...." Ray opened a folder and took out 8x10 photos. "Acting on information received we made a raid on premises known as "Cute Curls" including the flat above in Charminster where it was believed illegal drugs were being supplied. On entering the premises with legal search warrant, we found you, Marie, to be the only occupant of the premises. " Ray fanned out photos as he spoke. "Inside the premises we discovered ten kilos of heroin and the equipment and bags for making small parcels for distribution to users."

Marie Franks leant in to her solicitor and whispered, the solicitor then telling us what was said. "My client says she was looking after items for a friend and had no idea that the items were drugs."

Ray had heard that before and continued unfazed. "As well as the drugs we collected cash to the sum of ten thousand pounds, three Rolex

watches, two Louis Vuitton handbags, a Dolce and Gabbana scarf and ha
a dozen bottles of Chanel No 5."

Again, the whispered instruction to the solicitor. "Gifts from grateful clients."

Ray had to laugh at that. "Clients in Charminster buying Rolex? What, they travel over from Sandbanks for a perm?" He left a long pause and a stare at Franks to make it completely obvious he didn't buy it. "And ghost clients?.... Because the appointments book in the salon is virtually empty. Or are they your 'special' clients? Like the one who was with you when we arrived?"

The solicitor was quick. "To have an alternative lifestyle of sexual preferences is not a crime, Superintendent. I doubt whether Miss Frank's companion has made a complaint or that you are charging him with anything."

"Back to the drugs. We've had the salon under observation for several days. Distinct lack of hairdressing going on but a frequent stream of visitors, in and out quickly, and many known to us as users and sellers. A this moment, the ones we identified are being rounded up and brought in for questioning. I have no doubts we'll hear of you, Marie, providing drugs to them for use and resale. Anything to say?"

"No comment."

"What about Joseph?"

This had an effect. Under her heavy make-up I could see Franks pale.

Ray continued. "Oh, yes, we know about Joseph. He's a person of interest in the murder of Mariana Gosling. You knew Mariana, didn't you, Marie. Joseph is your backer and supplier. At the moment, we are only looking at charges of supply but with the Mariana Fox murder, we may be looking at accessory."

At this Franks broke her silence. "I had nothing to do with Mariana's death. OK, I was dealing but I wouldn't have anything to do with murder."

Her solicitor put a hand on Frank's forearm to rein her back and calm her, before speaking to us. "Are you going to charge as accessory or is that a scare tactic, Superintendent?"

"At this moment in time, no. But obstruction of our investigation into the murder and your client's relationship with the man, Joseph.....well, we can't rule it out."

Ray, unobserved, tapped my leg under the table – my cue.

"Marie, I'm investigating the murder. It may be possible to keep the two things in separate channels. But you need to help us find Joseph and before he kills again. Have a word with your solicitor."

The two women were almost head touching with whispers back and forth, while Ray and I leaned back in our chairs to give the impression of some privacy. We waited. Eventually, the women sat normally and the solicitor spoke.

"Is there a deal on the table, if Miss Franks assists your enquiries, Detective Chief Inspector?"

"With the amount of drugs and the current climate, the Crown Prosecutor would probably be unwilling to drop any charges but I could speak on Miss Franks behalf regarding sentencing, provided we get full and comprehensive co-operation."

The solicitor looked at Marie, who nodded, then began talking.

"I used to work at the salon, doing hair, and I had the flat above. The pay was terrible and I started to do skinflicks – that's how I met Mariana.

Harmless stuff but one of the photographers asked me out and they offered to pay for a bit of domination. It was good money and he introduced me to others, so I made the flat into a bit of a dungeon and advertised. Clients would pay more if I could come up with drugs – marijuana, coke – when we had sessions. It was easy to wait at the railway station and spot the County Line boys getting off the train. I soon had a regular and he would deliver to me at the salon. Then one day, Joseph turned up. I thought he was into the dom scene, being so big and strong. But he offered me a deal to make tons of money. His boys were getting picked up and he wanted a base in the area to bring his drugs direct and distribute from. It seemed so easy and how's a girl to get rich and get out of here? That's all I wanted. Enough money to go somewhere new and set up a proper hairdressing business – upmarket – and make a fresh start. "

"I understand, Marie. Tell me more about Joseph."

"He wanted local connections for getting the drugs in and I told him I knew a friend who might have someone who could do it. So I contacted Mariana and Martin Fox came over to meet Joseph. I wasn't in the room while they talked, I was making drinks in the kitchen when I heard Martin cry out. When I went back in his arm was bleeding and Joseph was holding a knife and a red candle. He'd cut Martin then poured hot wax on his arm. I thought it was dom scene but then Joseph started chanting something before cutting his own arm and pouring wax on. He never flinched. It was as if he couldn't feel any pain. I was scared. "

"Do you know Joseph's full name? His address?"

"No. He only ever said he was Joseph. I have a mobile number for him but it's gone dead."

"Let me have that, Marie. It may help us anyway. When did you last see him?"

I noted down the dates and intended to take them back to Phil Harding to put on his timeline.

Ray spoke. "Is there anything else you want to tell us, Marie? While you've got the chance?"

"The drugs and cash are really not mine. I was merely an agent handling the in then out. I passed the money to Joseph and he gave me commission. The watches and handbags were collateral on what customers owed but didn't have the readies."

"I suspect we are going to find that they are stolen goods and you've been handling."

"Fuck, no. I had no idea. Please."

"I think we'll let that go by for the moment. OK. Interview ended" and that was it.

CHAPTER 27

We'd made some progress with the interviews – strands were coming together but we still had a mystery man and no hard data on him. It's on Forensics to find fingerprints in the hairdresser's flat and maybe we can find on file. I phoned Phil Harding and told him what we'd learned and asked him to get on to CCTV footage from Charminster. With the dates we might be able to spot the Audi saloon, get a number, and possible clearer images of Joseph.
Detection now was heavily dependent on the technology guys to come up with evidence.

I detoured to a cafe and had the All-Day Full English. I was starving and not sure when I would get another chance for a hot substantial meal. I asked for the bacon to be crispy and the eggs to be cooked on both sides, extra toast. Tea came in mugs.

I decided I should take a chance.

I stopped at a General Store and bought two bottles of wine – one red, one white. I decided against flowers – just a bit OTT. Rather than phone first I would just turn up and see how it went.

Parking round the corner, if I had to leave later, bottles emptied, I could get a taxi and come back in the morning for my car. If I got to sleep over, I'd be sober in the morning and happy

A mid-terrace in a nice neighbourhood. The small front garden was tidy and rose bushes dominated the space. The bag with the wine bottles chinked against my leg as I walked the few steps up the path to the front door and rang the bell. I was nervous while I waited.

Eventually the door opened and I faced someone I hadn't expected to see. It wasn't Jason Statham.

"Hello, Max. I didn't know you were back."

"Harry. I came home this morning." and Max called over his shoulder, "Petra! It's Harry." before walking back to the lounge.

Polly came out of the kitchen, wiping her hands on a tea towel. She wasn't delighted to see me. I walked away from the door and stood by the gate so she would have to come out to talk.

"Polly?" I didn't have to ask the question.

"I know, Harry. He's asked me to take him back. He's been through therapy and says he's a changed man. He just wants another chance to make it up to me."

"Do you know what you're doing? Have you forgotten what he is like."

"Harry. He's my husband. We have to give it a go."

"I can make him leave, Poll."

"No, Harry. I have to take the chance it will work this time. Anyway. What have you called for?"

"Uh...I thought we could talk over the case. I was going to fill you in on how the interviews went... But, never mind. We can do it at the station in the morning."

I turned and left and I could hear Polly close her front door.

The assistant at the General Store was surprised to see me back so soon.

"Forget something?"

"Yeah. I'll have that fifteen year old Glenfiddich, please."

I wasn't ready to have an evening on my own so I went to Frank's place. He was surprised to see me. I didn't say anything but held up the Scotch and he stood back to let me enter.

"Glasses in the kitchen, Harry." He went into the lounge a bit quickly and I thought I saw him pick up a pill bottle and tuck it in his pocket.

I took two tumblers from a cabinet, unsealed the whisky and poured measures by eye before adding a single ice cube to each glass. The bouquet of toffee and honey notes raised anticipation. My father was standing by his music centre.

"Want to listen to John Field? One of mum's favourites."

My mother would play John Field's compositions on our piano. I felt that was too sentimental for this evening.

"Not tonight, Dad. Stick on some Chuck Berry." Dad is a big rock'n'roll fan. He selected a CD and slipped it into the player. Satisfied when Johnny B Goode started, he sat in his armchair and accepted a tumbler off me. I sat in the other chair. He only had two chairs – one for himself and one for a guest, usually Dave, or me when I found the time to call round.

He waved the glass under his nose and smiled. We wouldn't drink until half the cube had melted and cooled and diluted the spirit. He always drank his single malt that way and I had fallen in with it.

"Work OK?"

"Making some breakthroughs at last. Pieces falling into place."

"And your private life?"

"Still the same. "

Dad's silence was better than a question or comment. We listened to track two – In The Wee Wee Hours – while sipping our malts. On our third glass and Sweet Little Sixteen", my phone rang.

"Boss. I traced the car and put a call out with uniforms. Picked it up on cameras and it's currently parked at some derelict warehouses past the Town Bridge."

"OK., Phil. Text me the address. I can get there in ten. We'll keep an eye on it and see if Joseph is about. Contact Polly and Andy to meet us there."

"I'm already here, boss. There's no activity."

"What! OK, stay back 'til I get there."

My phone pinged with Harding's text of the location. Dad had overheard most of the conversation and understand when I told him I had to go, he could keep the whisky.

CHAPTER 28

The big guy was inside the warehouse for some time, Harding wondered if he had been noticed and the suspect gone through a back way, ditching his car. Or maybe he had a meet on. The boss would be there soon but maybe he should go take a look. It would be helpful to see if anyone else was involved before they had a chance to disperse. He couldn't let the opportunity slip through his hands. He felt he had a need to prove to the team that he could do the street and wasn't just a desk jockey.

Locking his car and pocketing g the keys, Harding carefully crossed the road and entered the yard. No sounds and nothing to see except an open door into the disused warehouse.
There was a risk that he would meet the suspect exiting so he created a strategy that he would be a guy looking for somewhere sheltered to have a pee, shrug and smile apologetically while handling his flies.

He approached the door with nothing happening, carefully stuck his head inside. No sign of the suspect but a tapping noise from deeper inside to investigate.....

CHAPTER 29

I pulled into the roadside and I could see Harding's Fiat Punto parked up but no Harding. I hoped he had got out for a better view and wasn't ash enough to enter the building after our suspect. My radio beeped; it was Polly.

"Boss. Armed Response are en route, with you in ten."

"Thanks, Polly. I can't see Harding, only his car. Warn the guys, two coppers in the vicinity."

"Roger that."

The only weapon I had was an extending baton, which I took from the boot of my car and held ready for use. I couldn't see or hear anything but I needed to find out where Harding was and team up with him. I didn't want AR mistaking him for our guy and a blue-on-blue.

The area was totally deserted, no traffic or people. Walking over to Harding's car, I was relieved to see he had locked it and taken the keys with him. No gift to an escapee. One of the small doors to the warehouse was ajar, the interior looking dark and uninviting, but that was where I needed to go. It was now obvious that Harding had entered the building as there was no cover in the yard and he hadn't seen me arrive. To say I was worried was an understatement..

Listening carefully at the door before squeezing in, I prepared for any attack, which never happened. The inside of the building was gloomy, a thin grey light weakly illuminating through dirty plastic roof windows. I sniffed the air. No cologne or cigarette smoke, fresh or stale, just machine oil and dankness. I could make out machines spaced out along the floor, remnants of the small engineering unit this used to be. On the ones directly hit by light, cobwebs indicated a lack of recent use. Listening, the only sound was the slow plonk plonk of a leaking pipe or tap somewhere. Over to my left was a large door to back rooms. To my right, an office, windowed so the foreman or boss could watch the operation. Disturbances in the detritus on the ground seemed to recommend I take the back room, which I did with the utmost caution. My chest tight and breath coming in short gasps, pulse pounding in my ears.

Through the open doorway, I could see Harding, motionless in a pool of his blood. I froze for a second then rushed forward to check on him but before I could reach him, a blow came down on my shoulder, the pain forcing me to drop my baton. Lying in wait, Harding as bait, Joseph had used a machete and I fell to the ground. He stood over me, sweat running down his face, his pupils dilated from drugs, probably cocaine. I could see the skull and snake pendant on a chain round his neck. He was a big man muscular under the light clothing he was wearing. Having lost the feeling in my right arm, I was unable to put up resistance, although I was aware of bleeding from the shoulder, the wetness creeping down my back.

"Give up, Joseph. You've nowhere to go. We know all about you."

"What do you know? Ha! I am the Voodoo Man. I'll change my shape and you won't know who I am."

"We'll always find you, Joseph. We found you now, we can find you again."

"But you won't be around to see it."

Joseph raised the machete, the dying evening sun sending a ray through a broken window and glinting off the steel, and all I could feel was regret. I'd failed. I couldn't save Harding or myself and the Voodoo Man was going to get away. I closed my eyes waiting for the chop.

There were two almighty bangs, deafeningly loud and echoing off the brickwork. I opened my eyes and saw Joseph had taken a double-tap in the chest and had slumped backwards against the wall but he still had fight in him. He pushed himself forward and I heard BAM BAM BAM until the click of a hammer on an empty chamber, starbursts of bloods erupting across his torso before he fell over my legs.

Someone spoke. "You alright, Harry?"

"Dad?"

Frank was standing over both of us, a worried look on his face and a smoking revolver in his hand.

"What the fuck?" I said weakly, what with blood loss and adrenaline overload.

"I followed you. Dave drove me. It sounded dangerous when you took the call. Jeez, son, you're bleeding hard." Frank dropped to a knee and examined my wound. "You're lucky. A thinner coat and that would have taken your arm off. Your woollen overcoat with the padded shoulders has taken the worse. Still, you've a deep cut but no arteries opened."

I started to think straight, despite the pain.

"Dad. You've got to get out of here. You shouldn't have a gun and you shouldn't be involved."

"A war souvenir, Harry. Thought it might come in handy one day."

"Clean it and throw it in the sea. Get out of here. Armed Response will be here any minute. Go, dad. I'll be OK. I can hear the sirens."

"OK, son. Just keep a grip on that wound." and he was gone.

I grasped my shoulder, kicked myself out from under Joseph, and tried to make my way to Harding.

"ARMED RESPONSE! NOBODY MOVE!"

"I'm a copper. DCI Harry Morgan. Get an ambulance. Men down." then I fainted, the last thought in my head was a prayer:

"it's a good day when everybody gets to go home."

CHAPTER 30

I was lucky, no permanent damage to my shoulder but I had a keepsake scar as a constant reminder to how close I had come to death. During my convalescence an Independent Enquiry ruled that Joseph had been killed by an unknown assailant, probably a gang rival. No murder weapon had been found and the bullets retrieved from his corpse had no history in Forensics. I gave evidence that I had not seen the gunman, being so wounded and looking at Joseph. With so little to go on, it became a Cold Case, unlikely to be handled unless new evidence turned up. Frank assured me that a fishing trip out in the Channel had been successful, despite not catching any fish.

I thought back to that night. What if I had gone in Polly's? Got the call there? Being at Frank's had saved me. My mind would spin and twist trying out the computations. I declined a trauma therapist but hit the bottle a bit hard. Again, it was Frank who watched over me and eventually I was fit enough to return to work.

As I walked back into the office, all the gang stood and applauded, which was terribly embarrassing. Polly gave me a huge hug; Andy looked like he wanted to. I gave a palm down hand wave to say "enough" and walked into my office past Harding's empty desk.

I sat there for what seemed ages, but was probably only a couple of minutes. My desk was clear, someone had tidied my mess. Polly came in with a mug of coffee and sat down opposite while I sipped at it. Eventually we talked.

"How you doing, Harry?"

"I'm not sure, Polly. It all feels like an almighty fuckfest. We didn't really get our man, did we?"

"Upstairs are happy we solved the case."

"So am I and Harding collateral damage?"

"No. Not at all. You did your job. So did Phil. It's what we all do and what we all risk."

I sighed, looked at the ceiling then back down at Polly, shaking off the self-pity.

"What have I missed?

"Not a lot. It's been quiet. The Met have followed up on Joseph and been wrapping up his network. Apparently there was another Joseph who was a voodoo priest. Our guy stole his name and persona. It seems a lot of people are happy he is dead. He was quite a bad influence on his patch. Andy's been leading a team on top end burglaries. A lot of break-ins at Sandbanks and Canford Cliffs."

"All under control then. Not much for me to do."

"Enjoy that. It won't last."

"Thanks, Poll."

Polly smiled and took away my empty mug. I found I was suffering shortness of breath, felt closed in.

"I think I'll take a walk. "

I didn't explain and left the office and the building a bit quickly. A short walk to the cliff top where I could suck in some fresh air and feel some early year sunshine. The sea was sparkling below. I felt I was at a crossroads and didn't know which way to take. There was something I needed to do... go visit Rose-Marie and Craig Harding.

I'd only spoken briefly on the phone with Phil's parents, what with my surgery, convalescence and too much time looking at the world through the bottom of a glass. With some trepidation I walked up their garden path and rang the doorbell. Craig answered.

"Harry. Come in. Come in. Rose! Harry's here."

Rose-Marie came out of the kitchen, drying her hands on a tea towel before putting her arms around. We were both crying. Craig gently pushed us into the lounge.

"I'll make us some coffee."

Rose-Marie and I sat together on the settee, holding hands. She spoke first.

"How are you coping, Harry?"

"Having the occasional flashbacks, Rose. How's Phil doing?"

"The doctors are pleased with his progress. He has a metal plate in his head where his skull was fractured and he'll have a scar but, thank God, he's alive."

"Would it be alright if I visited him?"

"He'd like that. He can't speak properly at the moment. He'll need a lot of therapy and we have to wait and see if there is any long term damage."

"I'm so sorry. I..."

Craig entered carrying a tray of coffee.

"Harry. We're so glad he's alive. You too. We must be patient. He has the best doctors."

"He cracked the case. His skills were the key factor. Without Phil, that guy might still be out there, ruining lives with drugs, killing others."

"We're proud of him. He loved working as a policeman and he was never happier than when he was in your team."

The rest of the visit was sharing memories and looking at photos of Phil as a young boy and student, then a constable. It was a cleansing occasion for me and I walked a little taller and straighter when I left.

As I got in my car, my mobile phone rang. It was Andy.

"Hi, boss. Where are you?"

"I've been visiting Phil's parents."

"How are they?"

"Doing better than I expected. Very hopeful of a full recovery."

"That's great. Listen. I'm calling to say you're wanted at HQ. The Chief Constable and the Crime Commissioner want you to attend at 1 o'clock."

"OK. I won't come back to the office. I'd better go home and have another shave and a cleaner suit. I'll let you know what they want later.

"OK, boss. Speak later."

What the F did this mean?

I'd had a shower and a complete change of clothing before heading out to meet the big bosses. Were they going to offer me early retirement on health grounds? Would I want that?

Or had something been found that implicated Frank in the death of Joseph? Had someone spotted him on CCTV in the area and recognised him? Waiting in the outer office to be summoned inside, I had to put my hands on my knees to stop them jumping.

Eventually the door opened and the Crime Commissioner came out with big smile on his face and offered me a hearty handshake.

"Chief Inspector Morgan. Good to meet you. Come inside. Would you like tea, or coffee?"

"No, thank you, sir. I'm fine."

"Good, good." He closed the door behind us and the Chief Constable rose from his desk and offered his hand.

"Harry. How are you doing?"

"Fine,sir. Arm a little stiff but otherwise no problems."

"How's young Harding?"

"I've just visited his parents. It's a slow recovery physically. His mental state will be evaluated later. I intend to visit him at the hospital later."

"Take our regards and our thanks. He'll get a commendation and possibly a medal. I know, I know. Poor compensation for his injuries but we need to show our appreciation somehow. Sit."

I wasn't sure whether I was being buttered up before they hit me with the bad news. The Commissioner sat in a chair, turned to me at right angles.

"Harry." he paused. "We didn't get this Joseph character before a judge but the murder was solved and a drug ring cleaned up. That's a good result."

"Thank you, sir. A team effort."

145

"Indeed. A team effort. But under your leadership. The Chief and I have gone over the files and the results of the Independent Enquiry. Exemplary police work. "

I was still uncertain where this was going. This was unfamiliar territory. The Chief took over the conversation.

"Harry. This county needs a Task Force. An elite team to head up the biggest cases. We're finding that there are more professional networks operating in Dorset. High end burglaries in our prosperous districts. Animal rustling on a big scale, not the local poachers.
We need to send a message that Dorset is not a soft touch, not all yokels.

The Commissioner finished the speech. "We'd like you to head up that Task Force."

I was temporarily lost for words. I had been prepared to be out of a job by teatime and now I was being offered huge responsibility.

"Uh. I don't know what to say. You've blindsided me."

"Harry. We have good coppers in Dorset but your experience and leadership skills put you at the top of the list. You've proved you work well with colleagues, with the Prosecutors and the Pathologists. People skills as strong as your detective skills."

"What do you expect of this Task Force?"

"Oversight of the big crimes. Collecting intelligence. Getting the co-operation of the different branches. The latter might be the hard part. People are protective of their patch."

"It's a clean sheet setup, Harry. Tell us what you would want."

"I pick my team. I'll take suggestions but I have the final say."

"Agreed."

"I want Andy Robins as second-in-command."

"OK."

"But he needs to be made an Inspector. He's ready for it and due it. I can't ask him to continue as a DS."

The two bosses exchanged looks and an unspoken communication. The Chief spoke, "I am sure that is possible."

"We stay where we are for now. Familiarity will get us off the ground running."

"Sounds good. You'll have the option to relocate but you'll be more mobile than you've been used to."

"I'll keep my team as is. I'd like DC Dave Wilkins on board.... And I want Phil Harding if he is fit to return to work."

"No problems with any of that. So it's a Yes?"

"Yes, sir. It's a Yes."

"Good man. Go back and unload any small investigations to other officers. Start with the burglaries that DS Robins is investigating. Put all your resources behind those."

A light bulb went on. People in Sandbanks and Canford Cliffs had influence. I would look at who had been burgled to see who had cried the loudest and been heard."

Final word from the Chief. "Any problems, you report to me. No one co-operates, let me know. Well, we won't keep you, Harry. Pleased to have you on board with this."

Printed in Great Britain
by Amazon

65550275R00088